FRIENDS CALL ME BAT

 This Large Print Book carries the
Seal of Approval of N.A.V.H.

FRIENDS CALL ME BAT

PAUL COLT

WHEELER PUBLISHING
A part of Gale, a Cengage Company

Copyright © 2019 by Paul Colt.
Wheeler Publishing, a part of Gale, a Cengage Company.

Wheeler Publishing Large Print Western.
The text of this Large Print edition is unabridged.
Other aspects of the book may vary from the original edition.
Set in 16 pt. Plantin.

LIBRARY OF CONGRESS CIP DATA ON FILE.
CATALOGUING IN PUBLICATION FOR THIS BOOK
IS AVAILABLE FROM THE LIBRARY OF CONGRESS

ISBN-13: 978-1-4328-5504-8 (softcover alk. paper)

Published in 2020 by arrangement with Paul Colt

Printed in the United States of America
2 3 4 5 6   24 23 22 21 20

DEDICATION

Authors who write historical dramatizations endeavor to portray history accurately. Fiction comes from animating the characters, but research is key to historical accuracy. This book is dedicated to all those who help us in that endeavor: visitor-center volunteers, archivists, museum curators, historical-site docents and guides, park rangers, and all those who work tirelessly in anonymity to preserve our history. We could not do our work without you. I've had the pleasure of working with many of you in the pursuit of my stories. To all those who have helped me or any of us who try our hand at history, I thank you. I hope this dedication says so properly. Our past might be lost without you.

This book owes particular debts of gratitude to Brad Smalley and Jerry Eastman. Brad is one of Dodge City's resident historians, whose advice helped me to a successful research trip. Jerry has impersonated W. B. Masterson for more than twenty years. His observations and suggestions helped polish this book to its final finish. My sincere thanks to both of you.

— Paul Colt

PROLOGUE

New York
1919

I'd never thought about telling my story this way. I never considered it much of a story. Some did. Magazine editors and a dime novelist or two created a little grandiosity with some of it. Newspaper editors more often had things to say, mostly hacking for some politician or reformer. Some were on my side but most on the side of those I opposed — like Otto Floto, that bloated bag of bovine flatulence. He never had anything good to say. Neither did I, of course, but that was personal.

It all started when young Runyon began pestering me with those infernal questions of his. He was always looking for a story. Persistent as a fly you can't shoo. I tried to ignore it. Mostly did, until that day I had lunch with Cody. He'd come to town with one of his Buffalo Bill Wild West Shows. I didn't care much for the show. Tried talking me into appearing in it, he did. Can you imagine? A portly newspaper reporter, gambler, ex-gunfighter, lawman appearing in one of his reenactments. Not a chance. I even turned down his offer of two ringside tickets. I'd seen that show already. Seen it when the bullets were real. I didn't need a theatrical reminder. Not that old yet. Good to see Bill, though, alive and kicking after all these years. *After all these years. Where have they gone?*

I suppose that's what set me to thinking. Put me in mind of a little nostalgia. That and we might have tipped one or two over lunch. Not many of our kind get to have reunions with old friends. Not many of our kind live long enough to be old friends. That alone cuts down on recollective sentimentality.

Runyon finally caught me in a weak moment, and the stories just kind of tumbled along from there. I figure they deserve a proper introduction. This one might have to do.

I was born November 26, 1853, in Quebec, Canada. My folks were farmers. I wasn't. We moved from Canada to Illinois and from there on to Kansas, where I'll take up the story. I was christened Bartholomew

Masterson. Never cared much for the name. Thought "Bartholomew" high minded and sissified. Nothing good ever ended in "mew." I changed it to William Barclay as soon as I was old enough to get away with it. I thought it more dignified and less dandified than my given name. I went by the formal name W. B. Masterson most of my life, but friends . . . call me Bat.

CHAPTER ONE

Longacre Square
New York, 1919

I became partial to favored haunts after coming east to New York in aught two. We settled in Longacre Square. Broadway suited the New York Bat Masterson like a pair of freshly shined shoes. When I wasn't at my desk at *The Morning Telegraph,* or covering a fight at the Garden, you could find me at the Metropole Hotel bar for a drink after work or Shanley's Grill for lunch or a steak dinner. The Metropole had a Victorian elegance about it. The spacious bar attracted an interesting clientele: entertainers, gamblers, writers, sportsmen, underworld kingpins, and connected guys aspiring to appear legit. The Met was a place to see and be seen. Shanley's knew how to turn a prime cut of steak. It, too, had an atmosphere, less formal than the Met. Relaxed elegance might best describe

11

it, but it was no less appealing to denizens of the square.

My office at *The Morning Telegraph* was in walking distance of our apartment. Truth be told, I seldom felt the need to stray too far from Longacre Square; that's what they called it before the *Times* moved in and got the name changed. I never could decide if that was a good change or not. Those were exciting years. We watched as Mr. Edison's electric lights slowly transformed Broadway into the Great White Way. Made me proud just to be a part of it.

I admit to having become a creature of habit in recent years. Made it easy to find me if Emma or any of my pals needed to for any reason. Young Runyon settled into the crowd I call friends not long after he arrived in New York. He was from Colorado. A Westerner, I suppose, though the West hadn't branded him quite like it had me. I'd met him when he was a kid in Colorado. He remembered it; I didn't. That Bat Masterson made impressions on the impressionable. Still does, though more for what I was then than what I am now. These days I'm a little on the gray and portly side. In spite of that, the old reputation follows me like a shadow. I don't mind; it's come in handy more than a few times.

Damon Runyon showed up at the Metropole one day, bellied up to the bar at my elbow, and introduced himself, or, rather, reintroduced himself. He claimed to have met me back in Denver. Like I said, I didn't remember. Thin, long featured, and sober, he countenanced a dour expression as might be prone to crack if enticed to smile or provoked to rage. In truth, his disposition tended to jocularity, though he hid that when he wasn't in the act of humor. Humor is probably what made us get along despite the difference in our ages. Humor and his insatiable appetite for stories of the Bat Masterson I once was. He might have made a modern version of that dime novelist Ned Buntline, except Runyon cared more for the truth. Buntline cared not a fig for truth. If the truth wasn't sufficiently sensational for Buntline's taste, he'd season it with imagination until it suited him.

Runyon wore his hair — some indistinct dark hue — slicked back. He favored suits that made a statement, ties, too, with a gaudy gold stickpin. He wore round, wire-rimmed glasses framing pale-blue eyes. They gave him a phony professorial appearance. Never far from his trade, he carried a note pad and gold pen in nicotine stained fingers that sported a pinky ring. Yes, a pinky ring with some fake stone. Anyone who knew Runyon knew him for a man too tight fisted to have expended real bucks on his adornments. I thought the pinky ring pandered to the more ostentatious preferences of his connected-guy "associates," as his hoodlum pals were known. I kept my opinions to myself, apart from the occasional admonition to avoid inadvertent self-incrimination. I had my drink. He ordered a cup of coffee to go with his cigarette, and we took a table.

The kid — in truth he was forty-one — was a kid to me nonetheless. Came to New York from some small Colorado daily. Caught on with Hearst and did right well for himself in the newspaper business. Covers sports mostly. Baseball? I tolerate it; worth a wager. Football? Spare me. Can't for the life of me understand folks' affection for that game. Hulky guys banging heads, covered in mud, battling for possession of a misshapen pig. Runyon covers it, too, along with the ponies. My game is boxing — the manly art of pugilism. Can't get enough of it. That's why the *Telegraph* hired me, and that's what I do, as we shall see. I do stray off the fight game from time to time when one of my favored topics trips my fancy. I won't bother you with those just now. You'll find out soon enough.

14

Runyon garnered my respect for his war correspondence. He went to Cuba with T.R., though attached to some Minnesota outfit. He went into Mexico with Pershing in '16 on the hunt for Pancho Villa. He didn't talk about it much; but between desert heat, mountain cold, every insect and serpent known to man — not to mention tainted food and water — Runyon thought Mexico a paradise. Near a year of that, and they never saw hide nor hair of Villa. I had to laugh. He was a bandit and a murderous revolutionary, but, try as they might, the U.S. Army couldn't put a rope around him. It reminded me of Geronimo; you have to respect that kind of cunning.

The Punitive Expedition turned out to be the opening act for Runyon's coverage of the Great War. I was already too old for either of those scrapes, but I admire the men who served. Don't think much of those who went out of their way to stay out of the way. That starts with our pinhead Professor in Chief, Woodrow Wilson. He irked me and every other American with red blood in his veins. He was perfectly content to sit on the sidelines until he had no other way to take a prominent position on the post-war world stage other than joining the conflict. There was no shortage of yellow-belly dodgers in

15

the fight game, either. I exposed more than a few of them in my columns at the time. More than a few, but Runyon wasn't among them.

It didn't take long to figure out what the kid had on his mind. He was in the newspaper business all right, but that was just a day job to support his writing habit. He thought himself a poet. Poetry didn't pay; baseball and boxing did. He also wrote stories, fictional stories; they were his passion. He was always looking for ideas. He got them from real life, he said. His search for stories led him to hang around with the city's underworld crowd. That worried me some, but he managed to keep his nose on the clean side of the pavement. There was that bet on the Willard-Dempsey fight that troubled me, but that came much later. At the moment, I guess I looked like real-life fiction, too.

He picked at me with questions about the old days in the West. I mostly just smiled and feigned an old man's loss of recollection. I liked him in spite of it. He must have liked me, too. He kept coming around with his questions. Occasionally he even asked me for advice. Advice is about all an old man has left worth giving. I'd never had a son; I felt honored he'd ask. I gave what I could, and that seemed to be enough. Then Bill Cody came to town. We reminisced over lunch, and, next thing I knew, Runyon had me with his questions. Nostalgia. It's a disease of the aged; I guess I'm infected.

Metropole Hotel
Forty-Second and Broadway
Late-afternoon sun muted to blue shadows in the city's concrete canyons. Little more than warm glow dusted the polished wood, glassware, and bottles arranged along the back bar. The after-work crowd lined the bar rail. I retreated to my usual corner booth. The first Tom Collins had just warmed my belly when Runyon made his entrance. He did make entrances.

He signaled the bartender for his customary coffee. He'd become a teetotaler after being wrestled to near ruin by a personal battle with John Barleycorn in his younger years. I admired a man who could conquer his demons.

"How was Buffalo Bill?" He pulled up a chair.

"Still Cody. A little older. Bigger than life even on his own stage."

"I suspect he might say the same of you."

"I'm not given to the stage."

"It must have brought back memories."

I nodded.

"Care to tell me about it?"

Right to his questions. He must have sensed weakness. The waiter arrived with his coffee. He lit a cigarette.

"I'll make it easy. I'll toss out a subject: just tell me whatever it brings to mind."

I got the drift. He knew my public story well enough to send me off in any direction he wished to go.

"If you know so much as to do that, what's the point of adding my ramblings to your file?"

"The public record, of course."

"Public record?"

"Is it accurate?"

"Oh, that. I suppose that is fair. Some of it has, shall we say, been embellished."

"Some of it?"

I felt the witness subject to cross-examination. "Most of it in one way or another."

"And is it complete?"

"I just told you: it's been exaggerated."

"That's not what I asked. Is it complete?"

"The public record? No."

"There is the point to your ramblings, as you call them."

I took a drink in resignation.

"Buffalo," he said.

My gaze drifted off to clear air, beyond the perpetual fog of tobacco smoke. Different haze. Dun dust rising against a clear, blue sky. I remembered.

CHAPTER TWO

Sedgwick
Kansas Territory
October 1871

I was just shy of eighteen. Built solid at five foot nine. Thick muscled in the arms and chest. The Almighty gave me the eyes. Mountain ice I called them, with thick thatch for a brow. Ladies liked them well enough. Men I faced soon learned to respect them. Brother Ed and I left the Sedgwick family homestead and headed south to hunt buffalo. We headed south to Stone's Store, where we signed on with a hunting outfit headed to Buffalo City in need of a couple of hands to finish out their season. We each had a Sharps big fifty and a sure shot to go with it. We expected to make our fortunes in buffalo hides. We were also kids. We soon found out you get started in the hide trade as a skinner. Nasty work skinning, but the work was steady and found kept your belly full. They put us to work running stock and skinning kills.

The outfit was pretty typical. The hunter headed the crew and did the killing. The crew consisted of a lead skinner, stockman, watchman, and cook. Each man drove a four-horse hitch wagon. All of us, except the hunter, worked as skinners.

I remember the first time we came onto a herd. We'd set off on a southwesterly course from Buffalo City. Three days out, we'd seen nothing. Then one morning the hunter lifted his chin to the horizon. "There they is," he said. Buffalo hunters didn't make their living on grammar. I didn't see any buffalo. About an hour later, you could see a thin, dun cloud, hugging the horizon like the lead edge of a storm. The closer we got, the higher and wider that cloud grew. We came to the base of a ridgeline. The sound of buffalo bawling filled the air. We rode to the top of the ridge overlooking a valley cross-hatched in creek bottom. You couldn't see the creeks. You could guess at them from where the trees grew. The valley floor was covered as far as the eye could see to the north and west in a thick carpet of wooly brown. I swear you'd run out of numbers before you got an accurate count on them. But what would be the point of trying to count when "endless" would do? Herds were like that in those days. This was but one.

The herds were quiet and serene browsing at their pleasure. Not so when riled up. The buffalo is possessed of a natural mean streak. Bad enough by itself, deadly when spooked. I've never experienced an earthquake. Read about them. I got a pretty good sense I know what one feels like, though. You get nearby a buffalo stampede with one of those big herds, you think it's an earthquake the way the ground shakes. A million pounding hooves will do that with a thunderous rumble that settles in a man's gut. That's your signal to get away and get away fast. This herd this day made a picture of tranquility. We moved in for the hunt.

The crew set up on a stand at dawn the following morning. The stand made killing brutally efficient. The hunter and others like him identified the lead cow in a herd. Buffalo are matriarchal. They go where mama goes. Once a hunter had a bead on the lead cow, he'd bring her down with a lung-shot. That shot would stop her in her tracks without killing her right off. The herd would mill around their fallen matriarch with no notion of flight. The hunters then systematically slaughtered them at their leisure. The business returned three dollars a hide at twenty-five cents a shot. The big fifties used a three-inch shell loaded for short, medium, or long range. If a new lead cow emerged, the hunter would bring her down in similar fashion to the first, and the slaughter continued. A competent hunter could bring down two hundred kills or more in a day.

The skinners went in with the wagons when thirty or forty were down. The herd would move some distance away, followed by the hunter to some new stand. Skinning made for grizzly work. You scored the hide around hooves and neck, then slit the legs to the shoulders and hind haunches. You loosened the hide at the hump and shoulders until you had enough to secure a good grip with a rope. With that accomplished, a mounted stock man dallied the rope to his saddle horn and peeled the hide off the carcass. Hides were loaded into the wagons for transport to base camp at the end of the day's hunt. There they were scraped clean and staked out to dry. The carcasses were left for carrion, with only the choicest meat, tongues, and an occasional hump taken for food.

Eastern and European markets for buffalo hides grew with demand for warm robes, coats, hats, and gloves. Railroads encouraged hunting both for the hide freight it produced and the fact vast wandering herds made mischief with train schedules. Get one of those big herds on the tracks, and you could lose hours to schedule. The army protected the hunters when necessary out of the belief the surest way to keep hostile Indians on reservations was to destroy their ability to live off the land, following the herds. They took that chapter from General Sherman's philosophy of total war. He'd cut the Confederacy in half with it in the latter stages of the war of succession. In those days, as general in chief of the army, he meant to do the same to the plains tribes. It all made for a prosperous business until hunting and disease thinned the herds to near extinction. No one gave a thought to that at the time; the herds seemed numberless.

By most mid-afternoons the wagons were full. We'd head for the nearest base camp, where we'd clean and stake our hides to dry. Base camps usually brought several hunting parties together. It was good for safety in numbers. Whiskey peddlers and wagon-bed saloons served the camps. A man could get himself a drink in a tin cup and count on finding a game of poker or monte to while away the evening hours. I learned card gambling in the buffalo camps. I learned to count cards and study the men who play them — who bluffs and who could be bluffed, lessons that came in handy later in life.

You got to know folks in the camps. That's where I first met Billy Dixon and a young fella a few years older than me by the name of Wyatt Earp. Wyatt stood six foot and stretched one hundred fifty pounds over a lean, wiry frame. He had long, sun-bleached hair and a moustache in those days. Sober as a judge in countenance with cool, circumspect eyes near the color of my own. He'd already built some reputation for a competent man most would defer to out of respect. We got on right off; I liked him. That was easy. For some reason he took to me. He wasn't a back-slapper by any means, but we found we had things in common like courage, loyalty, and resourcefulness. Who knew then what that friendship would become? We were young, alive, and doing for ourselves. Tomorrow was always just another day.

Brother Ed and I did some serious growing up in the hunting season of '71. By the time the snow fell, we headed for Buffalo City with a little money in our pockets to see us through that winter.

Metropole Hotel
Forty-Second and Broadway
I drained my glass. The blue shadow of late afternoon had brightened to evening street light. Runyon was still there. Funny me talking about Wyatt taking an interest in a young fella back then. Little bit like I'd taken an interest in Runyon.

"I knew you and Wyatt went way back. I had no idea you went back that far."

"Long time," I said.

"Sounds like the beginning of a story."

"Your stories are short stories. This one don't qualify; it's a long story."

"A long story is nothing more than an anthology of short stories."

"You think you have an appetite for all that?"

He nodded.

I shrugged. "Let me know when you've heard enough."

"Deal."

You don't know what you're in for, son. Son. Don't make too much of that.

CHAPTER THREE

Shanley's Grill
Forty-Third and Broadway

Shanley's may be the best steakhouse in New York. It's the best on Broadway by my account. A man can't eat steak every night . . . or can he? I'd be willing to try. In the spirit of gastronomical exploration, I find my way here quite often. The Grill is a bit less formal than the rest of the place but still toney and tasteful. Like the Metropole, it draws a good crowd. Runyon can get talked into it, too. That's where we found ourselves the next time he tossed out a story line.

"How about the Atchison, Topeka, and Santa Fe?"

"How about it? Two-part story."

"Start with the first part."

"Summer of '72 . . . Hot, dirty, backbreaking. Fond memories of railroad building that summer."

"Railroad building? I find that hard to visualize."

I gave him the fish eye. "You brought it up."

"So I did."

Fort Dodge
Kansas Territory
1872

The cattle business boomed in Kansas in the early seventies. The Kansas & Pacific Railroad ran service to Abilene and established a railhead on the Chisum Trail. By 1872, Abilene had an advanced case of cattle boom fever. Longhorn herds came up the Chisum trail from Texas. Trail hands, cattle traders, and those who served their prurient needs prospered. The town was wide open. The saloons, gambling dens, and brothels of the so-called Devils Addition prompted one newspaper to opine, "Hell was open for business in Abilene." And, of course, the Kansas & Pacific Railroad did a brisk business in cattle shipped east.

None of that was lost on the AT&SF. They wanted in on the action. They set their sights on Buffalo City, which wasn't much more than a permanent buffalo camp at the time. That suited AT&SF just fine. The markets for buffalo hides were served by rail. Buffalo City promised a steady business in hides to get started. Joe McCoy created the cattle trade in Abilene with a little development. McCoy built stockyards and a hotel that catered to the cattle trade. The AT&SF started building southwest, figuring to position a new railhead closer to Texas on what became known as the Great Western Trail. By the summer of '72 they planned to lay track from Fort Dodge to Buffalo City.

AT&SF contracted with the firm Wiley & Cutter to lay the track. Turned out, the outfit was more than aptly named. The company agent was a man named Ritter, Raymond Ritter. He put out the word in Buffalo he was hiring for the season. They offered good money to attract the labor needed to lay track from Fort Dodge to Buffalo City that summer. Ed and I saw it for a better opportunity than another season of buffalo hunting, with less skinning required for the laying of rail. Terms of the deal were payment on completion. That should have made me suspicious, but I was no more than a kid back then, and my brother Ed might have been the most trusting soul in the territory at the time.

My mind wandered back to unpleasant memories of that backbreaking summer. We groomed roadbed, humped steel, and swung hammers under blistering Kansas sun. The work day started at dawn and ended at sundown. Where buffalo camps offered amusements with liquor and gambling, end-of-track amusements failed by comparison. It's not that entertainments weren't available; we were just too dog tired to take too much sport. There was also the problem of money. We got paid when the tracks reached Buffalo City, so, along the way, we were mostly broke. In buffalo camp, you could spend trade credit for hides.

Day after miserable day that long summer we poured our sweat and sore muscles into that steel ribbon from Fort Dodge to Buffalo City. When the last spike was driven, and payday rolled around, Ritter gave us two weeks' pay, claiming he needed to get the rest from the company. He boarded an eastbound allegedly on that errand. You guessed it — he never returned. We were out a hundred-fifty dollars each. The company claimed they'd paid Ritter, and we should take up our claim with him. They were wily cutters sure enough.

We'd been cheated. I didn't take to it. I did a slow burn that turned to deep-seated determination. I promised myself I'd get us our money. I didn't know how, I didn't know when, but I'd do it. Some how, some way, some day, I'd get us our money. We licked our wounds as best we could after that and took advantage of what Buffalo City was becoming.

The heart of Buffalo City was a general store operated by Bob Wright and Charlie Rath. They dubbed the trail passing their store Front Street in what proved to be a stroke of real estate genius. They did a brisk business in the hide trade. In addition to being a successful businessman, Wright became a power player in Kansas politics when he renamed the camp Dodge City in honor of some prominent Dodge. Some said it was the chief engineer of the Union Pacific. Others claim it was the commandant at the fort. Doesn't matter much in hindsight. Dodge City came into its own and did right well for itself.

That August, anticipating arrival of the AT&SF and the boom sure to follow, James Kelley freighted in pre-fabrications for a frame building he erected on the corner of Front Street and First Avenue. There he opened the Alhambra — saloon, gambling hall, and restaurant. Kelly, too, rose to prominence in Dodge City society, serving as the town's first mayor.

I didn't realize it at the time, but these

men were destined to have a profound influence on my life in coming years. Dodge City and Bat Masterson would grow up together in the lore of the West, though at the time most of my attention was taken up by figuring out where my next meal might come from.

By the time the AT&SF arrived, development was well under way south of the tracks with grocery and general mercantile stores, a dance hall, café, blacksmith shop, and saloons, Chalk Beeson's Long Branch being the most notable. What self-respecting boom town didn't need saloons? Actually, self respect had nothing to do with any town laying claim to a boom. I learned that lesson following one boom after another across the West, first dealing in law and order and later dealing in cards and other games of chance.

In the early years, the AT&SF shipped buffalo hides by the freight car to markets in the East and ports serving markets as far away as Europe. Hides piled up on Front Street awaiting shipment were given the sobriquet "Stinker" and for good reason. In the heat of summer even the constant Kansas wind couldn't blow the stench out of town. Hides did have one advantage when they reached Dodge — they were dead. Other than the smell, they caused little by way of civil disturbance. Such was not the case with the Texans who drove herds of longhorn cattle to the new railhead. They had more on their minds after weeks on the trail than simply lying in the street, though more than a few of them surely did that.

Boisterous cowboy enthusiasm mingled with strong drink, gambling, and the favors of our prairie flowers brewed up a recipe for trouble. More often than not those troubles were resolved at the business end of a six-gun. Those who catered to the cowboys' entertainment were more than happy to relieve them of their pay. It was only the cost of the damages that sometimes accompanied their entertainment that gave cause for concern. These practices preceded our experience in Dodge by events in Abilene, giving rise to the stern law enforcement and reputation of one William Butler Hickock, better known as Wild Bill. It wasn't long before the business community . . . I hesitate to refer to them as city fathers, for in those days there were few fathers among them. I digress. They ponied up cash to pay for enforced order, law, too, being in somewhat short supply where Dodge was concerned.

Early attempts at law enforcement attracted the biggest, meanest enforcer to be found. He came in the form of Bully Bill Brooks. Like Wiley & Cutter, Bully Bill proved aptly named. Brooks's brand of enforcement soon became more bully than law. The intent wasn't to cripple the cowboys or drive them away. The intent was merely to civilize their enjoyments for the benefit of property and innocent bystanders, to the extent any "innocents" could be found standing by. Bully Bill wore out his welcome and was soon enough replaced by a vigilance committee.

On the surface, a vigilance committee of concerned citizens seems a perfectly reasonable solution to problems of the common good. That is, until the vigilance becomes neither common nor good. The meanest, toughest hombre to be found had not exclusive claim on abuses of power. Eventually that would lead to the need for duly empowered, professional law enforcement, but that would come in time. In the meantime, a man had to eat.

Shanley's Grill
Forty-Third and Broadway
I pushed my plate back as Runyon dabbed his mouth with a napkin.

"Did you ever get your summer wages?"

I lifted a brow. "What do you think?"

"I think I wouldn't want to be Ritter."

"You've got more savvy than you let on."

"Thanks. I think. So?"

"I need a little air. Let's walk over to the Metropole for a drink, and I'll tell you the rest of that story."

We settled the tab and took a little cool evening stroll over to the Metropole. We found a table. I ordered a brandy. Runyon, his coffee and lit a cigarette. I lit a perfecto and let my thoughts float on a curtain of fragrant smoke.

Chapter Four

Dodge City
April 1873

The two weeks' pay Ritter left us with didn't take us very far. Ed got a job tending bar at Jim Kelly's Alhambra Saloon. I caught on with Tom Nixon in time to catch the end of his hunting season.

Tom was tougher than saddle leather and demanding enough for a city desk editor married to your ex-wife. Tom Nixon knew the trails and the seasonal roamings of the herds. The latter were heavily influenced by the presence or absence of water. Nixon learned his savvy studying the Cheyenne and Arapaho, who hunted the territories we did. At times it seemed as though he could read the shaggy beards' minds. In truth it was more about habits and an acute sense of smell. I was plenty lucky to catch on with him. It put enough money in my pockets that fall to see me through the winter.

By the time frosty ruts warmed into spring, I heard reports Ritter was in Colorado. I made a few inquiries and waited. Finally, word came. Ritter was planning to travel east by rail, on a journey that would have him passing through Dodge. I had it on good authority which train he would be on. I told Ed I planned to meet the train and collect the wages we were owed.

The day dawned bright and crisp. I donned my best suit — actually the only suit I owned at the time — along with a clean shirt and tie. After breakfast, I treated myself to a shave and trim at the barber shop. By the time I headed for the depot word had spread, I guess. A small crowd followed me up Front Street with a larger crowd of spectators waiting at the station. At first, I kicked myself for having told Ed. He was a bartender after all. The only stock in trade they had beyond strong spirits was gossip. By the time I reached the depot, my thinking had evolved. Spectators were also witnesses. Considering what I was planning to do, a couple hundred witnesses might prove useful.

I stood on the platform and waited. Some in the crowd attempted to engage me with good wishes. I nodded my appreciation but avoided making any comments. My instincts told me — I have no notion why — this was a moment where actions should take precedence over words. My pocket watch crawled toward the scheduled arrival time. To the west, a small dark smudge appeared over the distant track. It grew slowly, climbing into the blue vault overhead. The smoke plume flattened over the engine's belching boiler. A whistle blast announced the impending arrival of the eastbound. It prefigured a call to action. I adjusted the Colt on my hip, eyes west to watch the train approach. I could feel the crowd behind me, riveted on what they might see.

We waited. The train drew closer. It slowed, rolling into town. The engine drew level with the depot. Brakes squealed, billowing gouts of steam as the engine ground to a halt at the water station beyond the depot. The passenger cars parked beside the platform. I boarded the last car and started up the line.

I found Ritter in the second car, reading a Pueblo daily. With his head in the paper I had my gun in his face before he knew I was there. I must admit I took pleasure in his surprise and displeasure at finding himself upbraided at the point of a gun.

"What do you want?" he says.

"You know very well what I want. My

wages and my brother's wages," says I.

"Take it up with the company."

"We did. They paid you. You held out on us."

I grabbed him by the lapel of his jacket and jerked him out of his seat. I marched him down the aisle to the platform at the back of the last car with a send-off shove for good measure. On the platform behind the last car we faced an audience fit for a politician on a whistle-stop tour. Ritter must have thought he could use witnesses, too.

"Call the sheriff!" he screams. "He's holding me up."

"Dodge is a mite short a sheriff just now," I said.

The crowd laughed.

"You owe my brother and me a hundred-fifty dollars each for laying this roadbed last summer. Three hundred dollars. Pay up."

"Take it up with the company."

"We've already been over that. They paid you; you held out. Now fork over your wallet." I cocked the gun under his nose to give him a good look at the leaden halo awaiting his pleasure.

His eyes crossed over the muzzle. I suppressed a smile.

"The money's . . . the money's in . . . in my case in the car."

The crowd tittered, amused at the stammer.

I called Henry Raymond, a man I recognized standing on the platform. He climbed onto the car platform. "Do Mr. Ritter here the favor of fetching his case. Next car up, third row from the back, rack on the left." Henry disappeared into the car.

"Mind pointing that thing somewheres else?" Ritter says.

"I do," I says. The crowd laughed again.

Henry returned with the case.

"Open it," I says.

The case contained a change of clothes and a bundle of cash.

"Count out three hundred."

He did and handed it to me.

The train whistle hooted.

"Now give the scoundrel his case."

He did and hopped off the eastbound, in which he had no further interest.

"Now get back to your seat, Ritter. If I ever see your sorry face again, you best be saying your prayers."

I stepped off the train as she began her roll up the track. Ritter ran into the car like a mad mama grizzly was after him. The crowd give up a rousing cheer. I led them off to the Alhambra, where I would give Ed his pay and let him buy a round for the house.

Metropole Hotel
Forty-Second and Broadway

I swirled the dregs of my brandy in the snifter.

"That's quite a story," Runyon said. "Did you ever see Ritter again?"

I shook my head.

"All's well that ends well."

"Did I say it ended there?"

"You said you never saw Ritter again."

"I didn't. But that was only the beginning."

"Beginning of what?"

"All the talk about me taking up the law in Dodge."

"And did you?"

"Not right away. Charlie Bassett was elected Ford County's first sheriff in June. He served four years before I got that star."

"So what did you do?"

"That fall I went back to buffalo hunting with Tom Nixon. Mean work was better than no work; but that's another story."

"Lundy's for lunch tomorrow?"

"You like that place?"

"I do."

"It's a deli."

"It is. It's a New York deli."

"It's a deli."

"You said that. You can't call yourself a New Yorker if you don't appreciate fine deli."

"Fine and deli strike me as oxymoronic."

"Please. It's just lunch. Spare me the pedantic lecture."

"I don't know if I should go slumming with your hoodlum pals."

"Slumming with hoodlums? Hell, you'll fit right in."

"I need to consider my reputation."

"Your reputation precedes you."

CHAPTER FIVE

Lundy's Delicatessen
Broadway, New York

Sun glare on the glass storefront cast the counter, cases, servers, and patrons in silhouette. The place was a madhouse at lunch time. Belly to bumper the lunch crowd shouted orders and tendered payment in a scene reminiscent of a trading day on the stock exchange down on Wall Street, trading in sandwiches no less. Twenty-four hours a day Lundy's dished deli cuisine to the denizens inhabiting Broadway and its environs.

Runyon ordered his usual pastrami on rye and coffee. When in Rome. I added a dollop of potato salad. It saved me fretting over menu choices. It's not like I couldn't stand the place; I just couldn't figure why Damon found it indispensable to his daily habits. He led the way to a back corner booth, which passed for quiet, as far as possible.

He slid into the booth against the back wall and unwrapped his sandwich with a gigantic pickle. I glanced around before taking my seat.

"I don't get it," I said.

"Get what?"

"What causes this chaos to charm you so?"

He glanced over my shoulder, eyes alight, and swept his arm over the scene.

"This is quintessentially New York. It's the city. It has a pulse. You can feel it here."

"Actors, hoodlums, hustlers. They're the underside of the society we call New York. They're not the people who make the city work."

"They're the people who make my stories work. Like you."

"Like me. Your stories are fiction; my story is not."

"Not yet. For now, it is inspiration. You were about to go hunting with Tom Nixon."

I was indeed. The prospect of exchanging bedlam in this present asylum for expanses of wide open prairie lifted my spirit to the horizon.

Kansas Territory
November 1873
The wind cut sharp lashes, laced in sand, buffeting hard. I grabbed my hat. I'd forgot-

ten how that wind felt. If the chaotic sur-
rounds of a New York deli struck me as
unrelenting, they paled beside the battering
onslaught of a Kansas wind in late autumn.
The herd we had on the stand moved on.
Tom and the rest of the crew headed back
to camp with the day's skins loaded on the
other wagons. They left me and my wagon
to clean up the last of the skinning.

Intent on my work, I took no notice. The
attack sprang upon me from behind a
nearby hillock. Five mounted Cheyenne —
from Bear Shield's band, I later found out
— bore down on me from behind. They'd
closed to lethal range by the time I felt pony
hooves beat the ground. They'd gotten close
by following the tree line along the bottom
of a nearby creek. They caught me too far
away to reach my Sharps.

The Cheyenne were proud warriors. By
their lights, we'd invaded their hunting
grounds. They meant to make a message of
me. Probably best they did, for it likely
saved my life. They lifted my pistol and skull
busted me with the butt of my own rifle. I
got a bleeding scalp, a headache, and a
double dose of embarrassment and humiliation. On the bright side, at least I kept my
bleeding scalp.

They took the wagon, hides, and as much

meat as the wagon would hold. They left me with a strong sign to get out of their hunting grounds. I ran for camp. Made it not long after sunset. I suppose I deserved the derision Nixon and the rest of the crew heaped on me. I'd lost the hides, my rifle, a pistol, and the wagon and needed patching up to boot. I was in no mood for abuse, having been grievously misused by the ambush. I argued we should mount up and go after the hellions to recover that which was ours and exact a full measure of revenge. Nixon would have none of it. The season was coming to an end. Our losses he reckoned not worth stirring up Bear Shield's whole band. Let them winter on the notion they'd bested us. Easy enough for Nixon to say; he counted his profits. I, on the other hand, bore the burden of indignity.

I rode a wagon box back to Dodge unable to shake the feeling of a tail having been tucked between my legs. It didn't feel right; I hated it. Nixon and his crew could do whatever they would. Bat Masterson wasn't taking this lying down; I did not lose like that. Losing could become habit forming; I had no tolerance for it. Bear Shield and his warriors might take to their winter camp with the notion they'd won, but I knew they hadn't heard the last of me.

By December, younger brother Jim joined Ed and me in Dodge. I convinced Ed to help me take retribution on the Cheyenne for my humiliation. You couldn't have kept young Jim home from that adventure with a posse.

Winter travel on the plains is hard and dangerous. Get caught in a big storm and you could end up marooned until spring or more likely frozen or starved to death. Young hot bloods such as we were don't assess natural risks with the respect more experienced plainsmen doubtlessly would. We should have, but we saw ourselves as above such dangers. We were impervious to natural hazards, or so we thought. As it happened, fortune smiled on us in our errand of daring vengeance. Perhaps as a testament to the indomitable spirit of youth, we got away with it. In later years, luck like that would have had me cleaning up at the tables. Come to think of it, the take on this run wasn't all that bad, either.

Bear Shield's winter camp wasn't hard to find. My plan was simple in concept. Run off as much of the pony herd as we could get away with and sell it. Simple, save one detail: how to do it? We hid the horses and Jim in a willow break upstream from the camp and went off in the long shadows of dusk to reconnoiter.

The camp sprawled along the banks of a shallow river, in the shelter of a low ridge to the west. Fifty or sixty tepees glowed like lanterns, lit from within by their lodge fires. It makes for a remarkable sight — islands of life set in harsh and desolate surroundings. The occasional dark figure could be seen moving about the camp or silhouetted against the light from a lodge fire within. The pony herd dotted the hillsides downstream from the village. We moved down the back side of the ridge to get a closer look at the herd.

He was easy to spot — a big paint, standing sentinel, his nose to the wind. He had to be the dominant stallion, owning the affections of the mares and the deference of the lesser stallions. A pale moon on the rise frosted his coat and the backs of the browsing herd.

"That's him." I lifted my chin.

Ed nodded. "He's the one. What do you think?"

"I think we move tonight. Nothing to be gained by waiting around to be discovered."

Ed tossed his head to a heavy bank of dark cloud building in from the north and west. "It may snow."

"I smell it, too. All the more reason to

make our move."

"How do you plan to play it?"

"We come in downwind from the east. I'll push across the stream on my horse easy enough the herd accepts me. Soon as I get a loop on the stallion, we make our run north. You and Jim push from the swings. If we can get enough of them, it'll cut down on chances of pursuit."

The moon climbed higher in the east as we crossed the river upstream from the camp and picked our way down the willow breaks on the river bottom. A northwest wind built in, advancing the chill that would bring us a storm. By the time we drew rein in a copse of trees south of the village, clouds had overtaken the moon.

"Best get to it," Ed said, his words formed in steamy, white vapor.

I nodded. "You and Jim wait here. When you see the herd start to move, that will be your signal to cross and push them along." I lay low on my horse's back, lariat in hand, and nudged him into the stream.

We circled the herd to the south and up the ridge wall toward the stallion. He browsed winter grass, pricking his ears to night sounds or lifting his head to test the breeze with flared nostrils. I eased closer. He picked up his head and inspected me with interest. We held still. My horse dropped his head to nibble some grass. The stallion lost interest and went back to cropping. We moved closer. The dance repeated a few more times before we joined up, and I got close enough to get a rope on him. The next time he lifted his head, my loop snaked out and caught him. He snorted in surprise. He stomped and reared, throwing his head. I dallied the rope to my saddle horn and led out up the ridge. He followed with a bellowed call to the herd. The mares picked up after him, following by the herd pecking order.

Ed saw the herd start to move. He and Jim crossed the stream and pushed up the ridge from the left and right swings. I picked up a lope. Herd mentality took over. We cut our way across the ridgeline headed north of the village. I expected the village would be alerted to the herd moving. They were. Shots were fired, either in alarm or in some futile attempt to stop us.

We splashed across the stream on a northeast track for Dodge. We lost a few head to water, as I expected we might. It took only a few mares to slow down the lesser stallions. It would take the Cheyenne some time to catch them, but they'd have mounts to pursue us. That, too, was to be expected.

After that, it was all up to time. Could we put enough miles between us and pursuit to get away with the stock?

As night wore on and the miles rolled by, snow swirled out of the black, featureless darkness. Large, lacy flakes at first, the stuff of a child's fairytale. Wind built in. Lacy flakes hardened to small, wind-driven sheets. A new race was on: now we had to outrun both our pursuers and the storm. The small hours of that night should have given me pause to consider the peril of our predicament. It should have, though I cannot remember it doing so. In truth, there was nothing else for it save pushing on.

The storm grew in intensity throughout the night. By gray light near dawn a thick blanket of snow had fallen. The snow abated; the wind did not. Drifting slowed our pace considerably. Horses tired quickly with their exertions, forcing us to pause frequently to rest. With nothing to browse, holding the herd with three riders proved difficult. The only mitigation to our dilemma came from the exhaustion of the horses themselves. We cut a creek near daybreak and stopped to water the horses. Ed rode in for a parley.

"I don't like it," he said. "We've left a trail a blind man could follow, and now we're slowed down to a walk."

"If we're slowed down, so are any Cheyenne that might be coming down our back trail. As long as the snow holds out we should be able to hold our lead."

Ed squinted into the gray gloom. "If snow is to be a blessing, it looks like the Good Lord has more in store. Let's hope it ain't more than we can push our way through."

"Odds on that won't improve by lollygagging here. Get back on your swing."

We pushed on through that day to another creek. Picketed the stallion with water and graze to hold the herd. We didn't risk a fire, but we managed a few hours' sleep. The snow calmed down to light flurries by morning when we pushed out again.

With the wind at our back, we made decent time. Whatever pursuit Bear Shield's band might have mounted must have gotten swallowed up in the storm. By the time we drove our prize up Front Street to the city corral, we made quite an entrance. With the herd secured we headed for the Alhambra to thaw out with a drink.

Nixon saw us come in. He bellied up to the bar at my elbow.

"Fine lookin' herd you brought in. Odd time of year for rounding up wild horses."

"It is, isn't it?" I said, more interested in

liquid warmth for my chills.

"We aren't gonna have a band of angry Cheyenne on the prowl lookin' for 'em, are we?"

I gave him the Masterson brow. "Not likely. They're mostly walking."

Lundy's Delicatessen
Broadway, New York

I wiped my lips on a napkin. The pastrami wasn't half bad after all.

"What did you do with all those Indian ponies?"

"We sold them. Twelve hundred dollars kept all three of us comfortable that winter."

"Did Nixon ever take you hunting again?"

"He did."

"I expect you stayed plenty clear of Indians."

"Not by a long shot."

"Don't tell me . . . let me guess. That's another story."

"It is."

"Metropole after work tomorrow?"

"If you're in need of coffee."

Chapter Six

Metropole Hotel
Forty-Second and Broadway

Shafts of late-afternoon sun splashed across the polished bar with the five o'clock crowd lining the rail. I ducked into a corner booth and pulled the jovial din up to my chin like a comforter. A tall, cool Collins refreshed the heat on a warm summer afternoon, with a bit of a breeze stirred by the ceiling fans. Runyon slid into the booth, cup of coffee in hand.

"How can you drink hot stuff in this heat?"

"Heats the insides so it doesn't feel so warm on the outside."

"You could ice some tea or have a lemonade. You could even have one of these." I held up my glass. "If they left out the gin."

"I've a long night ahead of me. I need to stay awake."

"Going out with some of your pals to case a job?"

"That would make me an accessory. I'd rather hear about it."

"I'm pleased you keep your distance from the actual crimes, if not the criminals."

"I'm surprised you trouble yourself about my associations, seeing as how you are one of them."

"Precisely why I'm concerned. I have my reputation to consider."

"Yes, we're all well aware of your reputation."

"Not that one. I'm talking about here in the city."

"There's a difference?"

"There is."

"And what might that be?"

"Here I am a man of irreproachable character with an interesting past. Out there I was something quite different."

"Reproachable character?"

"Not by your standards."

"Dangerous then."

"Some thought so. Let's leave it at that."

He lit a cigarette and flipped through a pocket notebook.

"You went buffalo hunting with Nixon and weren't done with Indians, I quote, 'by a long shot.' "

"Billy Dixon."

"Who's Billy Dixon?"

"The greatest marksman I ever saw."

I let my thoughts return to the scene. The last vestiges of winter hung in the chill, gray air. The crowd smelled of wet wool mingled with wood smoke. Conversation grew to a low hum as the room filled to the tinkle of bottles and glasses.

Dodge City
March 1874

Nixon called a meeting at the Alhambra to talk over plans for the upcoming hunting season. He invited his crew along with the heads of a number of other crews. He was concerned the herds in western Kansas were thinning.

"All of us have a stake in the coming hunting season. Toward the end of last season, the herds were not as plentiful as they'd been in past years."

Heads nodded agreement from some of the other crews.

"I'm not interested in a slim season," Nixon said.

"What's to be done about it?" someone said.

"I propose we move the hunt south of the Canadian into Texas."

"Into Indian territory?" someone said.

Billy Dixon spoke up. "That'll play hell with the Comanche, Kiowa, and Cheyenne."

Dixon was a fine figure of a man. Solid, powerfully built, rock-cut jaw. He was a plainsman's plainsman; they didn't come any better. He was also known as a crack shot. I didn't yet fully appreciate how good a shot he was. I thought my own shot pretty fair. Nixon, too. But Dixon . . . I smiled. He spoke with experience as an Indian fighter. Nothing much ruffled his feathers, so him bringing up trouble with the tribes carried weight.

"That's why you're all here," Nixon said. "There's safety in numbers. If we go south together, even the Comanche will have to think twice about takin' a run at us."

"Twice maybe. Quanah Parker won't need no third think," Dixon said.

"Let him try then. Pack a few extra cartridges."

"Pack a wagon load."

"So, what do we do about trade and stores?" someone asked. "We'll be too far from Dodge for a regular supply camp."

The meeting attracted a small crowd that weren't all hunters. A. C. Myers, who ran a general store in Dodge, spoke up.

"If the camp's big enough, I'll supply it

and make a market in hides as well."

A.C. had taken note of Bob Wright's business and saw the chance of moving in on it.

Saloon owner James Hanrahan noted the crowd in Dog Kelley's Alhambra and took something more than casual interest in the proceedings. He had a saloon full of thirsty men who'd need a place to unwind.

"I reckon a camp that size calls for a saloon."

A cheer went up at that. Nixon's proposal got up some steam.

"So, who's in?" Nixon asked the room.

Heads glanced around.

"I am," Dixon said.

That was all it took. The crews all threw in.

April 1874

We headed south out of Dodge, fifty strong with hunters and outfitters. Spring settled on the plains in the span of that month. The hills rolled lush green in new growth, carpeted in wildflowers and patched in dogwood and redbud. We crossed the Cimarron into Texas on West Adobe Walls Creek. We followed the stream to the original Adobe Walls trading post, where a decade before the legendary Kit Carson fought his famous Indian fight. We set our base camp a half mile east, one hundred fifty miles south of Dodge City.

Thereupon the hunters set to hunting, and the outfitters set to outfitting. Day by day the hunters went out scouting for herds. There were occasional reports of Indian sightings but no hostilities. Each night the hunters would return to Adobe Walls and fort-up the wagons in a tight circle, secure for the night.

Week by week a trading post worthy of the name began to take shape. Sod buildings were constructed to house Myers's store and Hanrahan's saloon and restaurant. A spacious corral accommodated saddle horses and mules. By May, a second store was built to house Rath and Wright's hide trading operation, along with Tom O'Keefe's blacksmith shop. Rath and Wright seemed unwilling to cede their hide business to the upstart Myers. Competition proved good for prices.

We spent our free time at cards, horse racing, and shooting contests. You could wager on them all. That was where I got my first look at Billy Dixon's marksmanship. He'd take on all comers. Long rage, short range, big targets, small targets, speed, you name it. I bet against him a couple of times and lost. It wasn't long before the only takers he could get on a bet were his opponents. I don't recollect he ever lost.

Comanche Village
May 26, 1874
We'd seen some Indians, but, like I said, we had no hostile encounters. That would change. Years later I learned how all that came about. The Comanche chief Quanah Parker called his Kiowa and Cheyenne brothers to a council.

The son of Comanche chief Peta Nocona and a captive white woman, Cynthia Ann Parker, Quanah was a charismatic leader and respected warrior. He cut a powerful figure for a leader of the sort a confederation of tribes might follow. Comanche blood colored his skin and the set of his cheeks, nose, and broad mouth and lips. He possessed a heart strong for his people and the vision to lead them.

Quanah called for the tribes to strike against the white eyes waiting for the buffalo to come. He was joined in this sentiment by Cheyenne chief Stone Calf and his handsome son Stone Teeth. A holy man, Isa-tai, which means she-coyote genitals, also addressed the council. He must have been some sight for a coyote. He wore a cap of woven sage, his naked body painted yellow to signify true *puha,* strong medicine. His medicine, he claimed, would protect all those who followed him from the white man's bullets.

Well, that was about all anyone needed to hear. The warriors took the medicine man at his word. The council determined to drive out the white hunters camped at white walls. They painted their bodies and horses the color of the sun to ward away the white man's bullets. War rituals drummed up a fever for certain victory. Bad medicine I'd call it, but as events would unfold, nobody smelled snake oil when the drummer arrived.

Adobe Walls
June 1874

We should have known trouble was coming. Hunters came into camp, reporting skirmishes with Stone Calf's Cheyenne. They'd run off some stock and attacked our resupply freight wagons coming down from Dodge. No serious damage was done and no more than we'd expected coming down there to hunt. May stretched into June. Summer heat arrived with the force of a hammer beating an anvil. As June ran along, reports of hostile skirmishes became more numerous. Hunting parties came into camp

61

out of concern something bigger might be brewing. Of those, several decided they'd had enough Texas hospitality. If the heat, scorpions, and snakes weren't bad enough, hostile Indians in number added danger to misery. Some pulled up stakes and returned to Dodge City. By the twenty-sixth, twenty-eight men and Hanrahan's wife remained at Adobe Walls.

CHAPTER SEVEN

Adobe Walls
June 27, 1874

A fortuitous and somewhat mysterious disturbance in the night had everyone up long before dawn. Hanrahan woke us to report a damaged ridge pole in the saloon where many of us slept. We had no choice but to repair it before the cave-in grew worse. By the gray light of predawn, we were already preparing horses and wagons for the day's hunt. Morning sun raised a ball of fire on the eastern horizon. The Comanche and their allies burst forth from the flames with a chorus of war cries at the clarion call of a bugle.

They galloped across the plain, a magnificent wave rolling like prairie fire on clouds of red smoke; warriors mounted on their finest war ponies, armed with lances, shields, and rifles. Naked bodies painted vermillion, red, and ochre adorned in war bonnets, scalps, feathers, and charms. Two hundred at least, some said, or more Comanche, Kiowa, and Cheyenne stormed the compound, led by Quanah Parker and the Medicine Man Isa-tai.

We scrambled to fort-up in the two stores and saloon. The initial assault overran the compound almost before the doors could be shuttered, barred, and barricaded. The fight came fierce at close quarters, eyeball to handgun as the attackers battered the doors. A dozen men scrambled to the rooftops. Heavy Sharps rifles came to bear on Parker's band and their allies. The big fifties roared to devastating effect. Slowly the initial attack dissipated. The attackers were thrown back under a rain of withering fire.

Shooting died away. A thick fog of powder smoke hung in the choking confines of the saloon, burning the eyes and sulfuring air, nostrils, and lungs. My ears rang till I could scarcely hear from the roar of all those guns fired in close quarters. We took stock of our plight.

"Anyone hurt?" Hanrahan asked.

No injuries were reported in either of the stores.

"You think we run them off?" someone said.

Dixon spit. "They's re-groupin'."

Sure enough, the bugle sounded again.

"What're the Commanch doing with a bugle?" I asked.

"Likely some bluecoat paid for them havin' it," Dixon said as he shouldered his Sharps.

"And taught them to play?"

"Here they come," Hanrahan said.

The second onslaught bore down on us, pouring in rifle fire and arrows. The attacking fire was largely ineffective, while our big fifties inflicted a toll. A hit pony tumbled under its rider, the fallen warrior overridden by his brothers. Another brave hit by one of those heavy slugs pitched from his horse, mutilated by a mortal wound. The assault blunted before the attackers could close to quarters putting us in peril. The big fifties tamped down their fight once it became clear the yellow medicine worked better for some than for others.

The situation settled into a standoff. The sun climbed to full rise while we forted-up safely in three little ovens baked in Texas heat. Hanrahan doled out ammunition from stores as we waited to see what might develop. Tension ran as heavy as heat. Later that morning, Parker and five warriors crawled through the corral to within a short distance of one store. They rushed forward in an attempt to break down the door. The door proved too stout, and, while the men inside couldn't get a good shot, the party took fire from those forted-up in other buildings. Caught in the open, the attackers retreated. Parker himself was wounded, returning to cover.

Midday

Quanah Parker's Comanche and their allies had us surrounded. They poured steady fire on us to no serious effect save making a trip to the privy too chancy to take. Fortunately, we set out enough powder smoke to cover the necessity of relying on chamber pots. Our big fifties afforded superior firepower. In the hands of marksmen like Billy Dixon, Tom Nixon, and, to some extent, my own, the careless attacker who presented himself a target needed more than yellow paint to protect him. One such attacker proved to be the Comanche bugler, an army deserter Billy picked off trying to escape.

The stand-off settled into siege once again. We took some comfort in our circumstance for the time being. We were heavily armed, fortified, and well provisioned. We could hold out for some time should the Indians persist in their hostility. The question lingered: how long? How committed were our attackers to their purpose? We had no hope of relief from anyone who might know our circumstances. We could hold out, but how long was long enough? I took comfort from Dixon. The most experienced man among us, he seemed unconcerned.

2:00 p.m.

The Indians retreated out of rifle shot. Things settled down to quiet and hot. Damn hot on the roof, where Billy and I took our turn at the watch. Indian warriors will undertake audacious feats of daring in battle to count coup and show strong medicine. So it was with one warrior that day.

Stone Teeth, son of the Cheyenne chief Stone Calf, embraced his war medicine. He rode in across the prairie alone on a flashy Appaloosa stallion. Magnificent specimen of a man, gleaming copper, signed in yellow paint, war bonnet flying in the wind. Neither Billy nor I raised a rifle toward him, though either one of us might have taken him down. It would have been a sure shot for Billy.

"Look at that crazy son-of-a bitch," Billy said.

"Not crazy; courageous," I said. He was

indeed. We found out later who he was.

He slid that big App to a stop and leaped down. Lance and pistol in hand he charged a portal in Hanrahan's saloon. He shoved the gun inside and emptied it to no more effect than filling the place with powder smoke and explosive reports. When he'd shot his load, he ran for his pony. Swung up and wheeled away.

From below the roar of a big fifty pursued him. Somebody lacking our admiration for the man's courage must have taken offense to the lead rain he'd soaked on the premises. Down he went. His pony bolted. He got to his feet with a nasty blood spill that looked to be mortal in time even from our distant vantage. A second shot of some lighter caliber brought him to his knees. He turned back to face us, drew a second revolver, and put it to his temple. In final defiance, he sent himself to his grandmother's land. He was one tough hombre.

4:00 p.m.

The Indians stayed out of rifle range, abandoning temptation to waste ammunition. They showed no sign of breaking off the engagement. We took advantage of the opportunity to clear some bodies downwind of the walls. That's when we discovered the first of our casualties. The Shadler brothers were caught asleep in their freight wagon and overrun in the first wave of assault. They'd been scalped. Scattered as we were in the stores and saloon, no one missed them. Another of the bodies we dragged away was a black man with a bugle we took for a deserter. We gathered any serviceable weapons and ammunition that might have fallen from owners no longer in need of them. Most of the latter weren't worth much more than the fact gathering them denied the enemy an opportunity to recover them for use against us.

The day fled into blue shadow and evening. Campfires dotted the horizon to the north and west. They wanted us to know they hadn't gone anywhere and force us to maintain a watch through the night. For all the fight, we'd been spared heavy losses. We'd dished out plenty in the bargain, but not enough to send them packing.

"You figure they've had enough?" I said.

Dixon gave me a look born of experience that said more *hell, no* than *no.*

I felt my youth and inexperience exposed.

June 28, 1874
That night and the next day saw some comings and goings. Henry Lease volunteered

to ride to Dodge for help. He left just after nightfall. He might have run into two hunting crews that slipped into the Walls that night. The fact he didn't spoke well of his skill in avoiding unknowns in a hostile situation. Indian trouble made it too dangerous for those crews to stay out on the plains. One of them, a slight young fellow of about my own age, would become a lifelong friend. Bill Tilghman was a buffalo hunter and a crack shot in his own right. Young as he was he had something of a reputation when it came to fighting Indians. He told me the story as we whiled away our watch hours that night.

"Couple years ago, now, we was hunting over toward the nations at the time. We came back to camp one night to find we'd been raided. Stripped the place of our supplies, they did, and destroyed the hides we had staked to dry. My partners felt like we should head back to Dodge before the hellions came back to lift our hair in the bargain. Bullshit, says I. We'll do no such thing. 'Course they couldn't wait to know what we'd do for our plight. I sent one of the boys back to Dodge with a wagon. If he traveled smart through the night, he'd be back before morning. Off he went whilst the rest of us cleaned and staked the kill for that day.

"I put up with a lot of grumbling that night over accomplishing nothing more than making us an attractive prize for the marauders to come back and raid us again or do worse. I told 'em all to put a stopper in it. We'd see who come to regret the damage they done us.

"By morning the supply wagon was back. I shooed the boys out to hunt and took cover in a willow break with a good line of fire to our campsite. The boys went off grumbling about leaving me behind for buzzard bait. I knew different. I knew them raiders would come back, and I planned to have a merry reception waitin' on 'em.

"Morning passed to high noon before a lone rider showed his-self on a low rise southwest of camp. He set there watchin' the way they do, 'til he convinced his-self we'd gone off huntin'. Once he started circling his pony signal-wise, I knew I had 'em. I filled the spaces between the last three fingers on my right hand with cartridges, so I could reload fast with one hand. 'Fore you knew it, six others showed up on that rise and rode in. They hopped off their ponies and set about the previous day's mischief.

"I remember watchin' 'em. They was

laughin' and palaverin' and havin' theirselves great sport at our expense, or so they thought. I let 'em get clear enough of their ponies they couldn't get out fast. I had three of 'em lined up like ducks in a gallery. The second one no more than got a look around to the first one gone down when I planted him, too. The third started for his pony; he didn't get far. The rest scattered like quail for some rocks and a nearby stand of trees. Three of 'em made cover, but I got the fourth. The three that made cover melted into the plains, like smoke in the wind.

"The shoot was over by the time the boys come in from where they'd been huntin' when the shoot broke out. They figured me for dead. Four dead Injuns took 'em by surprise."

Then and there I knew Bill Tilghman had brass. Seven to one odds, and he doesn't even blink. Next thing you know it's three to one odds, and the three are on the run. He was a man you'd value at your back.

"What do you make of this situation?" I says.

"Hard to say. For now, I s'pect they figure they got us boxed in. I s'pose they do if they're patient, 'lessen we do something to make 'em rethink their medicine."

CHAPTER EIGHT

June 29, 1874

Tilghman's words proved prophetic, though none of us saw it for challenging the Indians' medicine. What we did see the next morning was a small group of Indians atop a butte nearly a mile distant from the walls. We didn't know it at the time, but that party included Quanah Parker, the medicine man Isa-tai, and Stone Calf, along with the Kiowa leaders. It was Hanrahan who came up with the idea. He nudged Dixon and lifted his chin to the butte.

"Think you can hit one of 'em, Billy?"

My jaw must have dropped. I looked at Tilghman. He just shook his head. Dixon squinted against the bright blue sky and shrugged.

"Likely a waste of powder and lead," is all he said.

"Come'on, Billy." Hanrahan wasn't about to let go. "What have you got to lose? Hell,

I'll stake you to the round. Bring down one of them hellions at this range, you poke a big hole in their medicine."

Dixon took the offered long-load round with another shrug.

Tilghman and I exchanged glances in disbelief. We watched Dixon set up the shot. He'd need to aim high and drop the slug on its target. A light breeze from the south entered the estimation. At that range, he'd need to contend with some wind drift in the bargain. Going back to my gambling days, I wouldn't have taken that bet at twenty to one odds. Maybe at a hundred to one, but it would have been a small wager. He tucked that big fifty-ninety against his shoulder and took his sight picture. Easy breath. Squeeze. The Sharps bucked. We held our breath for what seemed an endless moment before one of them silhouettes pitched from his pony and fell to the ground. A cheer went up. Dixon like to have the breath beat out of him for all the back slapping he got.

"I'll be . . ." was all Tilghman could say.

I've never seen the like of it before or since.

Butte

Man-who-eats-his-enemy's-heart dropped

from his pony. His body hit the ground to the muffled report of the white man's shoots today, kills tomorrow long gun.

All eyes turned to Isa-tai.

"Puha," Stone Calf spit. "Since you are *puha,* ride down to the walls and bring back the body of my son who lies dead in your protection."

Isa-tai scowled at the insult. "Speak to the Cheyenne dog who killed the skunk. He brought the evil spirit to destroy Isa-tai's medicine."

"Come. We go," Parker said.

Adobe Walls

We watched the Indians pull out. They were leaving, all right. The question was for how long. The thing that disturbed some of us was the fact you had Comanche, Cheyenne, and Kiowa fighting together. It was one thing to take on any one tribe; a confederation of all three had a different odor about it. Hanrahan put that card on the table.

"Looks like Quanah Parker has put himself together some kind of federation. Them red devils fightin' one another when they wasn't fightin' us kept the pressure off some. I surely don't know what to make of this development."

"They pulled out," someone said.

"We go back to huntin'."

Some of us weren't so sure. Hanrahan had a point.

"I'm pullin' up stakes for Dodge," he said. "Anyone care to come along?"

A few heads nodded. I looked at Dixon, as did Tilghman. Dixon nodded. If it was good enough for him, it was good enough for the two of us. We nodded, too.

We rode out under cover of darkness and headed east. If Parker's bands were looking for us, they'd be likely to watch the hunting fields to the west or the main trail north back to Dodge. We turned north a day's ride out and cut the Cimarron. We arrived back in Dodge July 17th.

Metropole Hotel
Forty-Second and Broadway

Runyon sat back and stubbed out his third cigarette. He glanced at his watch. It was getting late.

"Quite a story. With hunting done for the season early, what did you do?"

"Hanrahan wasn't the only one worried by Parker's confederacy. He got the army's attention, too. They called out Colonel Nelson A. Miles in command of the 6th Cavalry and 5th Infantry to hunt him. Army didn't do much Indian fighting without scouts. Miles recruited Dixon and Billy spoke me in, too. They call that campaign the Red River War."

"Did you get him?"

"Parker?" I smiled.

"Looks like another story. Lundy's for lunch tomorrow?"

"Too noisy."

"You'll never put your finger on the pulse of the city without going to Lundy's."

"Don't need to put my finger on the pulse of the city. I got my own pulse to worry about. If you're interested, I'll be having dinner at Shanley's tomorrow."

"See you then."

Dodge City
August, 1874

Colonel Nelson A. Miles took command of what became known as the Red River War. He needed scouts and reckoned Billy Dixon one of the best. He took me on, too, at Billy's recommendation. The job paid seventy-five dollars a month with bonuses for carrying dispatches through hostile territory. Decent pay, and you didn't have to skin anything in the normal line of duty. 'Course you did have to be mindful of not having your hair skinned in the line of duty, though I counted that even odds against the perils of buffalo hunting.

We marched out of Fort Dodge August 11th, eight companies of the 6th Cavalry and four companies of the 5th Infantry in column. Miles presented an earnest appearance, crisp and military in bearing with fashionably long sideburns and a neatly trimmed moustache. He comported himself a competent cavalry commander. The scouts served at the pleasure of Lieutenant Frank Baldwin.

Baldwin sent us west toward Adobe Walls on Miles's intended line of march. By this time Parker's confederation had fractured, with tribes scattering in all directions. Miles made Parker the object of his pursuit, reasoning that, if the Comanche could be brought to heel, the rest would soon follow. Under no circumstances could Quanah Parker be allowed to apply his considerable charismatic talents to reassemble another intertribal confederacy. As long as he was on the run, we afforded him little opportunity to rejoin his alliances.

At Crooked Creek, we came upon the camp of a survey party. Five dead, their bodies stripped and mutilated. Baldwin ordered a burial detail, and we continued west. On reaching the Canadian River, Baldwin sent Billy and me ahead to Adobe

Walls to alert the hunters remaining there to the scouts' presence.

The hunters welcomed our return along with the rest of Baldwin's scouting party. News of the fate of the survey party sobered them all. They'd taken comfort from Quanah Parker's confederacy disbanding, but the prospect of renewed hostilities drained the last of their resolve to continue the hunt.

August 20, 1874

Baldwin received word summoning him to rejoin Miles and the main column at Cantonment Creek. We set out August 20th accompanied by the remaining hunters at Adobe Walls, who reasoned the company of the army preferable to the depleted numbers holding fort at the trading post. To no one's surprise, Indian sign was fresh and plentiful.

Following the Canadian River, we surprised a small war party. The hostiles dispersed quickly after a brief skirmish. Baldwin dispatched me and another scout to advise Miles as to the sign we'd observed and the scouts' location. On that ride I came to understand the payment of bonuses for courier duty.

We rode northwest through still more Indian sign. Two men alone on the plain made easy prey. We needed to move fast with speed tempered by caution. The message we carried was only of value if we delivered it. We traveled by circuitous route around ridges and exposed skylines, along creek beds and river bottoms affording the cover of tree lines and undergrowth. We rode early morning, evenings, and through the night, celestial conditions permitting. Always alert to our surroundings and mindful of our back trail, I'll confess to feeling relief when we finally intercepted the main column.

At hearing our report, Miles turned his column southwest. They joined Baldwin and his scouts at Antelope Hill on August 24th. Sensing the possibility of a decisive encounter, Miles pressed his pursuit of the renegades through extreme heat and drought at no small price to the men and stock under his command. We covered one hundred fifteen miles by the 28th, sixty-five of them in two days. Suddenly seventy-five dollars a month, bonuses notwithstanding, paled to a pittance when measured against saddle burn, heat, hunger, thirst, and lack of sleep.

Two days later, riding with a scouting party in advance of the column, we encountered fresh sign in the hills leading onto the Staked Plains. We'd come a long, hard way and now faced a furnace worthy of Dante's inferno. We followed the sign. The trail led to the mouth of a draw. Baldwin drew a halt, considering his options. Dixon caught my eye; I nodded agreement.

"Beggin' the lieutenant's pardon," Billy said. "That draw yonder looks like a trap."

"My thought exactly, Mr. Dixon."

"Seems like we might hold here for the colonel."

"That might afford them the quarter they need to slip away. How strong do you make their numbers by this sign?"

"Not many."

He caught my eye. He didn't like the question and showed his displeasure with a brown stream of tobacco juice.

"Then again, Comanch ain't given to leavin' sign plain as this. More'n likely we're bein' invited to circumstances of an unknown and unpleasant nature."

Baldwin thought a moment. I'll give him that.

"The colonel believes we may be on the cusp of a decisive encounter. I shouldn't think to disappoint him. If we can provoke a firefight he may be able to support us from a position of advantage."

He scratched out a dispatch with our location, suspicion of an ambush, and intent to engage. He sent his missive to Miles and nudged his horse forward into the draw. Dixon shook his head, drew his Sharps from the saddle boot, resting the butt on his thigh, and rode on. I took his lead. We wound our way up a narrow defile. I began thinking we might have overstated the alarm. That's when the heights above on both sides of the trail blossomed in muzzle flash, powder smoke, and a rolling rumble of gun fire over-arched by a shower of arrows.

We dismounted and scattered to such cover as could be found on the rocky hillsides and in gullies. We returned fierce if ineffective fire. As we feared, Parker and his band had us pinned down. They likely hadn't counted on the fact the scouts were better armed than regular troops and mounted a more fearsome defense than they might have bargained for.

Dixon and I had been right about the ambush. Baldwin was right about the colonel. Two battalions from the main body soon responded to our distress. They charged the hills on both flanks, throwing the Indians to flight. The colonel's pursuit easily overran the renegades' feeble attempts to fight a rear-guard action.

The Indians' main body fled deeper into

the harsh, waterless sanctuary afforded by the Staked Plains. There they soon outran us in our exhausted condition. The colonel was forced to draw down his pursuit and with it dismiss his best chance of a decisive encounter.

CHAPTER NINE

Shanley's Grill
Forty-Third and Broadway

"That's it?" Runyon said.

"Pretty much."

"The Red River War. Hardly seems worthy of the name."

"Miles would claim establishing Fort Elliott put a stopper in the bottle. That, a bitter winter, and drought forced the tribes, including Parker's Quahadas, onto the reservation the following year."

"Strikes me as a sad end to a proud people."

"There was some sadness to it. Their way of life changed. Most survived it. A few, like Parker, actually prospered."

"Prospered?"

"Quanah Parker was a transcendent leader. He led his people in war and then led them to prosperity in peace."

"I've heard the name. Don't know much

about him. Did you know him?"

"At the time, only from the battle at Adobe Walls and the futile trail we followed in the Red River War. Didn't seem any reason to know more than that. Despite his best efforts, I still had my hair."

"So, what did you do after the war?"

"Hunting conditions improved after the Indians surrendered. Hunting camp moved to Sweetwater five miles east of Miles's new post at Fort Elliott."

"So you signed on for another season."

"Afraid so," I said, with some regret at the memory. I've carried the consequences of that season with me for the rest of my life. In youth we make decisions out of an abundance of exuberance; we learn wisdom later. Would I put myself in a similar position today? I'd like to think not, but that would be wisdom talking. Would I have done things any differently back then? I doubt it. I could see some of that in young Runyon. He had his connections to the underworld. I'm sure he thought himself in as much control of his circumstances as I had in my day. Circumstantial control, we learn, is an ephemeral, illusory thing. Now you have it; now you don't. When you don't, like me you're left to wonder what happened.

The new buffalo camp built out along the lines of the camp we'd built at Adobe Walls. Charlie Rath opened a hide trading supply outfit. Hunters opened an "account" on which they could borrow or trade. They were paid two to four dollars a hide "on account" until accounts settled up at the end of the season. Rath's enterprise was soon joined by O'Laughlin's restaurant and boarding house, a Chinese laundry, and several saloons served by a wholesale whiskey trader. Like most frontier outposts, Sweetwater had no organized government and no law and order.

The most elaborate of the sporting parlors was the Lady Gay dance hall and saloon. Owned and operated by Billy Thompson, younger brother of the notorious gambler and gunfighter Ben Thompson, the Lady Gay sported a full range of gaming entertainments and a dance floor complete with a bevy of approachable ladies. One of the Lady Gay belles, Billy Thompson's sometimes sweetheart, Mollie Brennan, attracted more than her share of admirers, myself among them. One of them, Corporal Melvin King of the Fourth U.S. Cavalry, stationed at Fort Elliott, fancied himself a top hand with a gun to go along with his irresistible appeal to women, or so he thought. Ben Thompson joined his brother in Sweetwater in the fall of 1875, presiding over one of the faro tables in the Lady Gay. Fortunate for me as events would unfold.

January 24, 1876

I played at the tables in the Lady Gay that cold January day. Corporal King played in my game. He played badly, emptied his pockets, and made up for it by drinking himself near senseless. At some point, he left the game and disappeared. I tired of the game and took myself off to supper.

When I returned later that evening, Molly affected herself most flirtatious and sociable. As I recall, she wore a lavender gown, lace frills in a fetching manner at the bodice. She had cinnamon curls and emerald eyes, with a merry, throaty laugh that came with a smile fair to melt a man's heart. I was smitten in the moment by the pleasure of squiring her about the dance floor. The twinkle in her eye and the turn of a hip surfeit to put a man in mind of the most sociable of pursuits. It mattered not that she may have been making a show of me for Billy's benefit amid some tempest to their longer-term relationship. I'll admit willingness to avail myself of such an opportunity when presented to a man on a cold winter's night.

We'd just finished a lively reel and sought to pause for refreshment when Corporal King stumbled in. Red-eyed, it was clear he hadn't stopped drinking at his earlier departure. He spied us across the room. I was just drawing back a chair for the fair lady when King inserted himself into our company. He allowed as how it was time for Molly to partake in the favor of his company and invited that I should move along. I declined his offer, pointing out that it was he who was uninvited and that he might serve himself well by returning to the rock he'd crawled out from under. He took the suggestion with a belligerent, red-faced scowl. Molly rose to step between us as King drew his pistol and fired.

Molly took his ball through the swell of her breast. The ball, passing through, next lodged in my pelvis. By that time I'd drawn my gun and shot the blackguard point blank through the heart. Both Molly and King succumbed to their wounds. I stumbled to the floor, unable to stand.

The crowd of onlookers included a number of King's comrades in arms, who took offense to my killing their corporal. I feared they might finish my own killing when, all at once, they found themselves frozen under the muzzle of Ben Thompson's Colt. No one of them doubted Thompson would dispatch any that wished to accompany King to his untimely demise. The fight drained out of them then and there.

Ben got me to the surgeon at Fort Elliot. The surgeon operated for the purpose of removing the bullet, though he held out little hope of my survival. I hovered for a time on the brink of passing beyond the veils of this life. For reasons known only to our maker, I survived. The Thompson brothers shed their remorse over Molly Brennan's Irish wake. Billy blamed himself for the tiff leading to the circumstances of our confrontation with King. Ben and I formed something of a bond over my debt to him, a bond that was to last for many years to come. Two months after my encounter with King, I rode out of Texas headed for Dodge.

Shanley's Grill
Forty-Third and Broadway
"And that explains the limp and the cane," Runyon said around a cloud of cigarette smoke.

"It does," I said. "It also explains the end of my buffalo hunting days and the beginning of my gunfighter reputation."

"And how much of that story is fact and how much is legend?"

I smiled a shrug. "I shall leave that for you to deduce. I shall tell it only as it happened."

"Lundy's for lunch?"

I rolled my eyes. "If we must."

CHAPTER TEN

Lundy's Delicatessen
Broadway, New York

It happens every August. That morning when the summer heat stranglehold breaks. The air freshens on a cool breeze that whispers of the change about to come. I felt it, walking down Broadway to Runyon's favored deli. Inside, the high-noon rush had yet to arrive. I planted myself at the counter for pastrami on rye with a signature kosher pickle. I claimed a booth to await my perpetually tardy pal, whose arrival would be further delayed by the afore-mentioned high-noon crush.

Presently Runyon found his way to the booth, juggling chicken salad on white, coffee, and a fresh pack of cigarettes.

"For the life of me, Damon, I am confounded to understand your attraction to this place. One could have a quiet lunch complemented by pleasant conversation and coherent thought within a stone's throw of this bedlam. All this for a sandwich with a side order of dyspepsia. Really?"

"It's New York, Bat. It's where the action is. How can you not love it? A man who once risked forty-five caliber lead poisoning for the price of a slice of apple pie."

"At least that poisoning was peaceful once the smoke cleared."

He shook his head to that with a bite of chicken salad, followed by a napkin dab to the chin. "Let's see . . . when we last left you, you were concluding your buffalo hunting days with a cane and a limp."

I escaped the din by mind travel back to Dodge.

Dodge City
May 1876

Dodge had changed by the time I returned, most notably from steady service by the Atchison, Topeka, & Santa Fe along Front Street upon, I must say, a masterfully constructed roadbed laid by the labor of my back and the sweat of my brow. The effect was to civilize the buffalo camp, if civility can be applied to buffalo camp turned railhead cow town.

Dodge sprawled east to west along Front Street bisected by the AT&SF tracks. Bridge

Street crossed Front at Second Avenue north and south, spanning the Arkansas River south of town. Broad plazas bookended the town with watering tank and freight house on the east opposite a stout timber jail south of the tracks. Dodge House stood on Railroad Avenue two blocks east of Bridge. The Iowa Hotel occupied the northeast corner of the plaza at Front and Third along with the post office and Wright and Beverly's store. Delmonico's Restaurant and Chalk Beeson's Long Branch Saloon, where Luke Short ran the gaming, meandered west along Front from First Avenue. Ab Webster's Alamo Saloon, City Drug, a gun store, James "Dog" Kelley's Alhambra Saloon and Dodge Opera House, and a barber shop were other notable additions. Saloons, gambling parlors, dance halls, and stock pens comprised the seamy, "anything goes" underside of society south of the tracks. Drunkenness, debauchery, brawling, and gunplay typical of an end-of-trail cow town displaced decorum south of what some called the deadline.

Cow towns were well understood by the time the AT&SF reached Dodge. Experiences in Abilene, Ellsworth, and Wichita prepared Dodge for the lawless arrival of Texas cowboys fresh off a long, dusty trail with itches to scratch, whistles to wet, and pockets full of paydays of which they might be relieved. In late 1875 the business community banded together to establish a rudimentary city government for the provision of law and order. Governance was politically divided almost from the outset by those who favored civil law and order and those who favored a more permissive atmosphere, allowing the visitors license to blow off steam while emptying their pockets. The latter faction, headed by Bob Wright, included Charlie Rath, "Dog" Kelley, and most saloon owners. This cabal, known as the Dodge City Gang, secured political control, though opposed by a law and order, reform-minded faction headed by George Hoover. The so-called dead-line figuratively drawn down the center of Front Street would symbolize the divide that would shape Dodge politics for years to come.

In April 1876 the city council adopted ordinances meant to secure a modicum of civil order. Among them were measures prohibiting animals on sidewalks or in business establishments, the wearing or discharge of firearms within the city limits, public intoxication, and offenses against public decency and tranquility. These provisions were enforced north of the tracks.

Business proceeded as usual south of the deadline. George Hoover was elected mayor and forthwith wired Wichita, summoning Wyatt Earp to a post as assistant city marshal, a position legend has promoted to that of city marshal. Wyatt served under Larry Degner and later Charlie Bassett, never advancing beyond marshal's assistant. Wyatt recruited my brother Jim as city policeman. I joined him in a similar capacity shortly after returning from Sweetwater.

Wyatt Earp and I were to become lifelong friends. We struck a bond forged out of abiding respect, good humor (mostly mine), and absolute trust in each other. The first thing to impress me about Wyatt Earp was that he was a man who did not know the meaning of fear. The thing we call courage is a complex brew. Men behave courageously by overcoming natural fear for the greater fear others might judge them cowardly should they be seen fearful. Wyatt cared for none of that. He measured himself by his own estimation. I do not believe the man ever felt a tremor of fear; he simply did what he expected of himself.

I remember one occasion in Gunnison, Colorado. Wyatt ran a faro concession at the time. Ike Morris, a local gambler with something of a reputation as a gunman, showed up to play at Wyatt's game while Wyatt was out of the saloon. Morris made a rather substantial wager, which he proceeded to lose. When the dealer collected his bet, Morris complained the deck was stacked and demanded his money back. The dealer deferred to Wyatt. When Wyatt returned, Morris made his demand. Wyatt consulted with the dealer, who assured him in private the deck was not stacked as Morris had alleged, whereupon Wyatt "admitted" to Morris the deck was indeed stacked. He said that, while he was inclined to give Morris his money back, he was concerned that the nature of Morris's demand might make this appear a sign of weakness. For that reason, he would keep the money. This turn of events left Morris to decide if righting the injustice was worth facing Wyatt Earp. He left that night and soon after departed Gunnison altogether. That was Wyatt Earp. Appearances counted. His was the only estimation of himself that mattered.

In Dodge Wyatt preferred managing rowdies with his fists or the butt of a gun. We adopted the practice of subduing unruly nuisances, rendering them senseless by a blow to the head with a gun butt or, in my case, the head of my cane. We wisely backed up these tactics by working in pairs with a watchful eye and ready gun at the back of the arresting officer. Our total trust for one another grew out of these confrontations. The gun was seldom called for. Even drunk cowboys knew by reputation no future could be found in tempting that fate. Wyatt's reputation was well founded. Mine took root within a short time following my arrival.

I only recall a couple of occasions in Dodge where Wyatt shot a man in the line of law enforcement. Tombstone was a different matter, but that came later. A dispute of uncertain origin prompted a drunken cowboy to ride his horse up on the boardwalk at the front of a variety theater, passing Wyatt in the dark as he was making his rounds. The Texan drew his Colt .45 and ventilated the clapboard theater in the direction of the stage. Wyatt drew and fired twice. The rowdy Texan pitched his last roundup. Word spread among the Texans along the Great Western Trail: don't mess with the law in Dodge.

Wyatt and I made good partners. I enjoyed his company, but I knew from the outset a man would never find his fortune behind an officer's shield. A sheriff might do well on account of tax collecting duties, but those were elected political offices not open to hired employment. The knowledge rendered me disposed to temptation when they discovered gold that summer in the Black Hills of Dakota Territory. Wyatt understood gold fever. He accepted my resignation graciously, and I headed for Deadwood.

Cheyenne
July 1876

I got no farther than Cheyenne and a run of hot luck bucking the Tiger at faro. I'd enjoyed gambling at cards in the buffalo camps. The streak I hit in Cheyenne delayed my travels to Deadwood. The world of wealth available at cards struck me as less arduous than panning for gold and attended by appreciably more opportunity for success.

All that of course proved true, so long as the cards turned in my favor. As we all know, runs of that sort have a way of running their course. By August my luck joined the party headed by lady luck and the fickle faith of her odds. About that time word began to drift south on a trickle of defeated gold-bugs, who reported the best of the gold claims staked out. I took stock of my situation. Faced with fall and prospects for winter, I decided in favor of steady found in the employ of Dodge City law enforcement.

Wyatt acknowledged my return with only a modest amount of "I-told-you-so" ribbing.

Lundy's Delicatessen
Broadway, New York

"So is this the official beginning of Bat Masterson, peace officer?" Runyon said.

"As good as any, I suppose."

"You and Wyatt have been friends for a long time."

"We have."

"Was this the time you became such close friends?"

I thought about it. We'd been friends for so long, I never really thought about where it all started. "We met back in our buffalo hunting days, but that was mostly in passing. I guess you could say we came to be good friends in our Dodge City law days. Having someone you can trust at your back in a tight spot will do that to a man."

"And you had him at your back?"

I smiled. "And me at his, too."

"Sounds like the next part of the story."

"I suppose it does."

Runyon glanced at his watch and drained his coffee cup. "Until then." He scraped back his chair.

"What's the rush?"

"Sister Margret Mary Claire."

99

"A nun?"

"She is."

"I never took you for a religious man, let alone Catholic. What would your gangster pals say?"

"Most of them are Catholic, at least nominally. They mostly leave religious practice to their wives and girlfriends, though."

I shook my head. "Gangsters, nuns, and a Catholic. Is there no end to your surprises?"

"I didn't say I was Catholic; I just lean that way."

"Hedging our bets are we?"

He smiled. "Maybe."

"And what's so urgent about your business with Sister-something Mary? They're all Mary-something."

"If you must know, I sometimes help with manly chores around the convent. This time it's a little car trouble."

"I never would have guessed you for nursemaid to a tin lizzie. Do you get stories from the good sisters?"

"Not yet, but you never know. Later."

CHAPTER ELEVEN

Dodge City
October 1876

My luck wasn't all left in Cheyenne. I returned to Dodge just in time for Ford County sheriff Charlie Bassett to take me on as a deputy, thus making me the logical choice to succeed him as sheriff, as he was prohibited by Kansas law from running for a third term. Wyatt and I once again found ourselves enforcing the law — he in the city marshal's office, me in the wider county jurisdiction.

Over the winter we readied ourselves for the summer cattle season. Those wide open cow-town days were the days a Dodge law dog earned his keep. My days as a buffalo hunter had made me proficient with a big fifty, a weapon of impractical use when it came to most law enforcement situations. I tended to favor Wyatt's buffalo approach to subduing the unruly. My cane served well in such situations, owing to a heavy brass knob. Still, in the law business, you couldn't rule out the use of deadly force. My unpleasant encounter at the Lady Gay had memorably taught me the value of lighter, faster fire power. That winter I outfitted myself with a pair of nickel-plated, short-barrel .45s finished off with gutta percha resin grips. In later years I indulged my sense of style with pearl handles, not easily overlooked when prominently displayed, and added the affectation of engraving. All of it suited my purpose. Backed by my notorious reputation, the mere sight of my conspicuous firearms coaxed reason to the lights of even a whiskey-addled cow hand.

For practical considerations of marksmanship, I ordered the guns mounted with a slightly higher, thicker front sight, reminiscent of my trusty big fifty. That sight acquired a target quickly even in the tightest of squeezes. I also specified a light trigger pressure. I reckoned these features more important than the speed of the draw. In a gun scrape the decision didn't necessarily belong to the fastest shot; the surest shot carried the day.

Serving under Charlie Bassett marked the beginning of what would become a multifaceted professional association and a long and eventful friendship. Charlie was one of the Dodge City old timers. He opened the original Long Branch in partnership with Al Peacock. In 1873, they elected him Ford County's first sheriff. Re-elected him, too.

The cattle season of 1877 was a busy time for law enforcement. It was also lucrative the way we kept the peace. Wyatt was dead serious on one point: gun play was an absolute last resort. As a result, the rowdy and raucous were subdued by buffaloing them. Buffaloing was a practice that favored imposing the rule of law by means of some blow to the head, rendering an offender unconscious. This might be administered most often by the butt of a gun, occasionally by a fist or, in my case, the heavy knob on my cane. We worked in pairs, with the buffaloing officer backed by the threat of a gun. Buffaloing was good for the business of law keeping. We padded our seventy-five-dollar-a-month salaries with two-dollar-fifty-cent arrests. Dead men didn't earn an arrest bonus; the buffaloed did. At the height of the cattle season, they paid at a rate of some three hundred dollars a month.

Buffaloing was also consistent with the pleasure of the Dodge City Gang political class. The saloon owners didn't mind their cowboy guests blowing off steam within reason. Dead cowboys didn't blow off any steam or empty their pockets in the process. We maintained enough peace and order with a rap on the head to maintain public safety without harsher measures as might make our visitors feel unwelcome. Still, word spread: don't mess with the law in Dodge.

Life was good in the season of 1877. So good I was able to put some money into an interest in the Lone Star Dance Hall. So the season passed to the prospect of a subdued fall and winter. Then things got interesting.

Shanley's Grill
Forty-Third and Broadway

"Let me stop you there for second," Runyon said.

We'd gone to Shanley's for a decent lunch. I indulged in a bite of Waldorf salad. Shanley called the concoction something else, owing to the Waldorf Astoria's claim of having invented adding apples and walnuts to a chicken salad, but a rose by any other name is still a Waldorf salad.

"I am curious about this reputation phenomenon you keep referring to."

"What's curious?"

"The ostentatious show of firearms. The

aura of notoriety. It's almost as though you wore it as a uniform to go with the badge."

I thought a moment. "I suppose we did."

"Did it work?"

"We thought so."

"Why?"

"Intimidation. Fear can be a more potent weapon than anything discharged from a firearm."

"Fear of a fast gun, then, was more effective than the gun itself."

"It could be."

"Were you? Fast, I mean."

I smiled. "People thought so."

"But were you fast?"

"Fast enough. Probably not the fastest, but fast mostly didn't really matter; accuracy mattered. A fast man who beat you to the draw and missed ended up dead. A deliberate man who didn't miss was most often fast enough."

He shook his head. "Did you bluff playing cards?"

I smiled again. "When I thought I could get away with it."

"So your gun reputation let you get away with bluffing law-breakers."

"It did."

September 1877

We received a report Sam Bass and his gang had robbed a Union Pacific train at Big Springs, Nebraska. They made off with a king's ransom, some sixty thousand dollars in gold double eagles shipped from the San Francisco mint. The U.P. and their Pinkerton guards wanted Bass bad. Reports had him headed our way. Charlie ordered up a posse, and we rode northwest hoping to cut Bass's trail.

Charlie knew Bass for a Texan. Reports speculated he and his ill-gotten loot were headed for home. We got as far as Eagle Tail Station, about a week after the holdup. Word reached us there'd been a shootout with the Bass gang at Buffalo Station in Nebraska. Two gang members were killed and some of the proceeds recovered. Bass was not among them. Buffalo Station was east of Big Springs. It raised questions in Charlie's mind about the accuracy of the reports we'd received on Bass. After a few more days of futile searching, saddle sores persuaded Charlie we were on the trail of a wild goose. We headed back to Dodge empty handed that time. We'd come to better result a little further down the line.

Bass got away. You'd have thought sixty thousand would have set a man up for a while, even more so when he was linked to robbery of a gold shipment bound for Cheyenne from the Deadwood Home Stake mine. That happened only a few weeks before the Big Springs train robbery. He hauled in twenty thousand on that score. Didn't matter; he was back in the train business the following year, this time in Texas. He gave the law fits for a spell. A former freighter, he knew every coulee, arroyo, and cow trail in that part of Texas. Rangers caught up with him in Round Rock later that year. He died in a shootout.

January 1878

Charlie Bassett endorsed me for sheriff in the fall campaign of 1877. That, of course, got me the backing of the political faction known as the Dodge City Gang, which basically meant the backroom power in Dodge. I won easily and was sworn in on the fourteenth. Not one to overlook experience, I appointed Charlie under-sheriff to serve with me.

Ford County stretched west from Dodge clear to Colorado, nine thousand five hundred square miles of unorganized territory. The jurisdiction defied law enforcement on the budget afforded by a county as sparsely populated as Ford County. When occasion arose, as it did soon after I was sworn in, we could call on competent posse men to assist. Wyatt, of course, was a ready hand. Bill Tilghman, buffalo hunter of the Adobe Walls fight, ranched near Dodge. My younger brother Jim had also come to town. Brother Ed served Dodge as police chief.

We'd scarcely taken office when we got our first call to trouble. On January twenty-seventh, Dave Rudabaugh and four accomplices attempted to rob a train at Kinsley, Kansas, in Edwards County. The attempt failed, and the gang fled. The AT&SF offered a reward of one hundred dollars a head for the arrest of those responsible. Edwards County law enforcement failed to apprehend the gang. The Adams Express Company, with offices in Dodge, asked me to take up the case. With five hundred dollars in reward money there for the taking, it didn't take much to raise a posse, even faced with the hardships imposed by pursuit in the dead of winter.

We rode out to the sand hill country hoping to pick up some trail sign or reported sightings. We got as far as Crooked Creek when a winter storm blew out of the north. I knew that country from my hunting days and remembered a cave and rock cove where we took shelter to ride out the storm.

Snow swirled on a howling strong wind through the night of the twenty-ninth and the following day. We had windbreak and shelter from the snow for men and horses. We found enough wood to fire a pot of coffee and a pot of beans, but blanket warmth was all that could be had in the way of comfort.

The storm afforded time to think. Unpleasant as the weather was, it suggested one possible advantage. If the bandits were in the area, they'd likely seek shelter, too. I reckoned they'd not know the country as I did, narrowing the choices they might make for shelter.

By the thirty-first, discomfort and the tug of a strong hunch induced me to abandon our shelter and brave the storm. We followed the creek bed through the snow to the Lovell ranch at the mouth of the creek. Much to my disappointment, my hunch didn't pan out, and we found no outlaws there. Lovell reported having seen no one before or during the storm. We took consolation in warmer shelter, prepared to ride out the storm in a nearby dugout.

As gray light faded toward evening, dark riders approached through the snow. Rudabaugh was known to me, as was Ed West, another desperado in his company. One of our number, Josh Webb, volunteered to entice them to shelter in the dugout. He stepped outside, waded through the snow to a tree, and relieved himself, pretending not to notice the new arrivals. Buttoning himself up, he greeted them with a friendly welcome, sympathizing with their plight at being caught out in the storm. They rode up to the dugout with Webb trailing behind.

I stepped out of the dugout, guns drawn in warm greeting. West lifted his hands; Dave thought about going for his gun. Webb cocked his piece behind the outlaws, giving Rudabaugh pause to reconsider. We invited them to drop their weapons and step down.

With the storm abated, we returned to Dodge with our prisoners the next morning. Rudabaugh was in surly spirits, more so when the steel bars of the cell door clanged shut behind him. The posse disbanded, though, with another three hundred dollars in reward money still on the loose, interest in the case remained keen.

A little more than a week went by when we got a tip that two more of the gang had been spotted near the Lovell ranch. I rounded up another posse, this time with Wyatt, Bill Tilghman, and my brother Jim. We reached the ranch and with Lovell's help picked up a trail southwest. We pushed hard, probably paining Jim some. Wyatt, Tilghman, and I could all be resolute when the situation called for it. A two-hundred-dollar pursuit called for resolute.

Winter tracking is easy as long as the snow cover holds. The farther south we rode, the more sparse snow conditions became. A week out of Dodge, sign got scarce in the vast tracts of the staked plains. Over a campfire on a bitter cold night beneath a sky that appeared a bucket of diamonds pitched on black velvet, Wyatt called the question.

"They've given us the slip, Bat."

Tilghman agreed.

I hated to admit it, but they were both probably right. We headed back to Dodge in the morning empty handed. Another week and five hundred miles of winter tracking behind us, we made it back to Dodge.

The case lay dormant until the middle of March. Charlie and I were in the office, around the fifteenth I think it was. Brother Ed came in with one of his city officers. Two members of the Rudabaugh gang had been spotted in a saloon south of the tracks. Charlie grabbed a sawed-off eight gauge, and we headed across town. The pair were gone by the time we arrived, though we obtained what turned out to be a reliable report that they'd ridden south toward the river.

We tacked up our horses quick as we could and rode south after them. The pair turned careless. We overtook them and had the drop on them before they figured out they were being pursued. I expect they thought they were in the clear after all this time. It made for quite the reunion when we locked them up with Rudabaugh and West. Four out of five wasn't a bad haul in the reward department, either.

CHAPTER TWELVE

Metropole Hotel
Forty-Second and Broadway

Rain splattered the cobbles in pitchforks and hammer handles. September can be like that. We'd taken refuge in the Metropole bar. It was still raining when I finished the Rudabaugh story. Runyon tamped a fresh pack of cigarettes on the table, packing the tobacco tighter before opening.

"So that was the end of Dave Rudabaugh. Lot of reputation for a failed train robbery."

"End?" I said. "Not by half."

"Did he escape?"

"Didn't have to. He turned state's evidence against his partners in June and walked when the matter came to trial. He departed to Las Vegas in New Mexico territory along with Josh Webb. They hooked up with a corrupt justice of the peace name of Hoodoo Brown. They formed their own Dodge City Gang of a different stripe and got on with the business of lining their pockets."

"Did you ever cross his path again?"

"I did. But that came later."

Runyon looked out the window, assessed the downpour, and ordered another cup of coffee. I risked another Tom Collins, figuring we weren't going anywhere anytime soon.

"Let's see . . . spring of '78 — that's about the time your brother Ed . . ." He let that touchy subject trail off.

"Died," I said.

He nodded. "Is it true, you avenged his death?"

"Dime-novel horse droppings. I didn't get there in time to avenge anything. Ed . . . Ed did right by himself. You make your living packing a badge or a reputation, you need to back it up. It takes courage, skill with your weapon, and you'd best be deliberate. Decisive and deliberate. I've seen plenty of men with courage and skill die for lack of the last. My brother was a good man. Nice man. Too nice. He'd rather josh and swap yarns than hold a man's toe to the line. Trusted folks to do the right thing. That kind of trust too often gets misplaced."

My thoughts drifted.

Ed and one of his officers, Nat Haywood, were making their usual evening rounds. Around ten o'clock they entered Josh Webb's Lady Gay Saloon south of the deadline. A cow outfit had hit town, and by that hour the boys were fresh full of flit. Ed detected a drunken cowboy named Jack Wagner packing a gun in violation of city ordinance. He ordered the cowboy to give up his gun; Wagner complied. The outfit ramrod, a man name of Walker, offered to check the gun for his man. Ed agreed and handed it over. That was Ed — too trusting. Bad mistake. Sometimes you have to pay that piper.

Ed and Haywood stepped outside to continue their rounds. Wagner and Walker followed them out. Ed noticed Wagner still had his gun. He called Wagner on it and ordered him to give it up again. This time Wagner refused. Ed attempted to take the gun; Wagner resisted. Haywood moved in to aid Ed. Walker pulled a gun and leveled it in Nat's face; the gun misfired. Wagner managed to draw his pistol and shoot Ed point blank in his right side. The muzzle flash set Ed's shirt on fire. Walker turned on Ed. Ed border shifted his gun, tossing it

115

from right hand to left. He staggered back, firing three times. He hit Wagner twice and Walker once; both wounds were mortal.

Ed made it back across the dead line to George Hoover's Saloon, where he collapsed. George got him up to bed. I got there quick as I got word. I found him in his room. Couldn't do no more for him than hold his hand for a time before he passed. Damn shame. A good man done in for a too trusting mistake.

Metropole Hotel
Forty-Second and Broadway
I sat for a time lost in the memory.

"Must have been tough losing a brother like that," Runyon said.

I had no answer, still alone with Ed in that room above George Hoover's saloon.

Runyon eyed a break in the rain outside. "I best shove off while the rain's stopped."

I nodded.

"See you next time," he said to a chair scrape.

I sat there for some time, remembering. We were kids. We went West together to seek our fame and fortunes hunting buffalo. Ed ended up tending bar and packing a star to make ends meet. Some fortune. I hadn't fared much better for all that. All things considered, I'd lived closer to the edge than Ed and for a lot longer. I managed to walk away in the end. Probably shouldn't have; so many of my kind didn't. Men I called friend succumbed to their appetites for chance and violence. Was I better than they were? Better than some; not better than a few. I give myself credit for knowing the difference.

Wyatt and I were about the only two left. Wyatt probably owed his long life to being that good. Me? I questioned myself long and hard after Ed died. I understood what did him in. I wasn't likely to make the same mistake as Ed. Not that one, but there were plenty more mistakes a man might make besides misplaced trust. Seen now, in a long-view reflection, I began to understand. I'd walked away not for having successfully avoided all the mistakes I might have made. I walked away for one simple reason I well understood: luck. It was luck pure and simple. I'm a gambler; gamblers understand luck. I had my share of it, good and bad. Bad luck cost me money; good luck let me walk away. As a gambler, you expect to break even. In the end, I guess I did, at least in that game.

Shanley's Grill
Forty-Third and Broadway

Bright sunshine sliced between buildings muted in shadow as I hurried down Broadway for lunch. A chill wind cutting through my coat had me thinking about a bowl of that French onion soup for lunch. Dry leaves skittered down the street, collecting in crunchy little piles caught in the cobbles. I swung into Shanley's and claimed a booth just ahead of the rush with a well-timed wait for Runyon to make his appearance.

I had my coffee cool enough to drink by the time he arrived.

"Sorry, deadline and all that, you know." He dropped into the booth.

I knew. "Good story?"

He signaled for coffee. "Backgrounder. Army-Navy game this weekend."

"Football backgrounder. Let's see: there's mud. Some blood. Sweat and, oh, yes, a pig given up its skin in the name of Neanderthal sport."

He rolled his eyes and lit a cigarette. "Football is an up and coming sport. Baseball is the national pastime, and you, my friend, have time for neither. The world of sport does not revolve around a boxing ring."

"It should. Manly contest. I'll risk a wager

118

on a baseball game."

"Football is a manly contest, too, not to mention the grand tradition of our rival military academies. It's pageantry. It's spectacle."

"It's boring. Leather padded men pushing, shoving, and grunting to advance a misshapen ball through a muddy pasture. Really."

The waiter arrived to concede me the point. I ordered my soup. Runyon ordered the special, shepherd's pie.

"I couldn't help reflecting on the unfortunate circumstances of your brother Ed's demise. Dodge was one tough town."

"It was tough, but you could have some fun with it, too." I had no interest in revisiting maudlin reflection.

"Fun? You mean the legendary Masterson humor?"

I smiled.

Dodge
1878

Bill Tilghman joined the city police force that spring. A man of action going back to his buffalo hunting days, ranching proved a trifle tame for Bill. Cattle season hadn't gotten under way as yet, so we sent Bill out on patrol by himself to get his feet wet. Awfully rainy that spring. Town was quiet enough until shots rang out on Front Street. Bill drew his gun and ran north toward the tracks. He skidded to a stop at the sight of a small fellow in a baggy coat and a high-crown hat walking down the center of the street, being pursued by two armed men intent on shooting him in the head. Bill barked out his challenge, and the two immediately put up their guns, whereupon the strangest thing happened. The little fellow pulled off his hat and stuck wiggling fingers through two holes in the crown.

"I won," he says.

Tilghman looked from the little fellow to the two gunmen in disbelief. "Won what?"

"Why, the bet," the hat man says.

"What bet?"

"The bet I could walk down the middle of Front Street without getting my hat shot off."

Bill holstered his gun. Later when he returned to the office I asked him, "Any trouble?"

"None worth arresting."

"Not even Luke Short shot in the hat?"

We had a good laugh on Tilghman over that.

CHAPTER THIRTEEN

Shanley's Grill
Forty-Third and Broadway

"Practical jokes with live fire," Runyon said. "Still sounds like a tough town to me."

"Not so tough. Luke had holes in his hat. The shooters shot blanks."

"Tilghman didn't know that."

"No, he didn't. Still made for a good one on him."

"Practical jokes are not the stuff of tough reputations. There must have been more to back up your story than that."

"I suppose you could say that." *Reputation.* I chuckled to myself thinking back on it. *Mostly it was fiction, literally fiction.*

"Don't make too much of those stories," I said.

"You saying Dodge wasn't a tough town?"

"Dodge had that reputation during the railhead years of the cattle drives. Those Texas cowboys came to town with their wild on for sure. Mostly it tended to be rowdy fun. They were just boys after all. We seldom needed our guns to deal with their troubles, except maybe to rap a skull now and then."

Runyon scratched his head. "But you and Wyatt Earp were two of the most notorious gunmen in the west."

"So they say. As a newspaper man you should know not to confuse notoriety with truth. If you do, notoriety becomes the truth."

"So, you're saying it isn't true about you and Wyatt."

"No. Wyatt had his share of gun scrapes. Take the George Hoy shooting." My eyes drifted. I couldn't resist a smile. "That one started about the time vaudeville entertainer Eddie Foy came to town to play Dick Brown's Comique, a gambling house and concert hall. Appropriate of a comedian, things got off to a comical start."

Dodge City
July 1878
Foy's arrival in particular afforded opportunity for good fun. Being a comedian and a flamboyant one at that, one could scarcely resist the opportunity to poke a bit of fun at his expense. Imagine his surprise, having recently arrived in town, when he

was seized on Front Street by a mob and hauled off to a tree with a stout limb fitted with a rope. Don't know if the man could ride or not, but he took on a look of pure terror when they set him up on a horse. Genuine panic set in when the noose settled around his neck. "What have you to say for yourself?" The rough ringleader says. "Where's the law?" Foy squeaks, whereupon I stepped round from behind the tree wearing a grin. The little fellow had a presence of wit about him. "Anything I have to say for myself," he says, "can best be said with a drink in hand." With full-throated good cheer the performer was rescued from his intended fate and delivered to the Long Branch saloon to plead his case before the bar by purchase of a round. Things got serious after that.

After Ed's death, the city council named Charlie Bassett city marshal. Charlie appointed Wyatt his assistant. Some two hundred fifty thousand longhorns and more than a thousand Texas cowboys made it up the Great Western Trail to Dodge that season. They arrived in town to find a company of professional gamblers, many of notorious reputation, ready to relieve them of their hard-earned wages.

The notables included Ben and Billy

Thompson, Mysterious Dave Mather, Luke Short, Doc Holliday, Virgil Earp and younger brother Morgan. It was up to Charlie, Wyatt, and me to keep the peace. When you think about that bunch and the fearsome reputations they bore, you imagine it a recipe for trouble. The gambler gunfighters were never a problem. None of them were involved in a shooting incident that season. None of them ever confronted another. Reputation bred its own code of respect.

The same could not be said for the cowboys. They were a rambunctious lot by nature. Dodge offered pleasures to all their appetites. When you mix cowboys blowing off steam with whiskey, women, and gambling, trouble was seldom far removed. For the most part troublemakers could be buffaloed by our usual tactics. A night in jail and the occasional fine sufficed to handle run of the mill offenders.

Serious law enforcement in Dodge wasn't popular with the Texans trailing herds to the railhead. They hated Wyatt in particular for his strict, no-nonsense law enforcement. That came to a head in the '78 season.

July 26, 1878
Eddie Foy trod the boards at the Comique

in the wee hours of the morning, performing to a full house. I was at one of the gaming tables. Wyatt and my brother Jim were making their regular rounds. A group of cowboys rode south for the bridge when one of them wheeled around and galloped up to the Comique gun in hand. He fired three shots that ripped through the clapboard walls. Foy dove out of the footlights. Doc Holliday, along with me and everyone else, hit the floor.

Outside on the street, Wyatt drew and fired. According to his account he missed when the rider's horse jerked away. The cowboy returned fire and spurred his horse for the river. Wyatt wheeled around, took careful aim, and knocked the shooter out of the saddle.

The offender, one George Hoy, would succumb to his wounds within days, but not before confessing he'd taken the opportunity to try to kill Wyatt for the thousand-dollar bounty someone had put on his head. Hoy's death would give rise to yet another legend soon after the season.

Shanley's Grill
Forty-Third and Broadway
Runyon motioned the waiter for a refill on his coffee. "So, Wyatt comes by his reputa-

tion honestly even before his famous gun-fight and vengeful ride. Are you saying your reputation wasn't justified by the Corporal King affair?"

"No. I'm just saying my reputation got overblown."

"You're just saying that."

I shook my head.

"Then how'd it happen?"

"You arrest those young cowboys. They sober up and go home with tales to tell. Mostly the tales get told so as not to make the teller out to be a fool or a coward. Tales get bigger and better with the telling. Some magazine writer who doesn't know the difference between notoriety and truth picks up a story; or, worse, a dime novelist gets the bit in his teeth. Next thing you know, you hear stories about yourself you don't recognize. Some said I had twenty notches in my pistol grips. Imagine — twenty."

"So none of it's true?"

"I didn't say that."

"Now I'm confused."

"A lot of folks are; puts you in good company. Better than the usual in your case."

"Maybe my friends' reputations are over-blown."

"That's a bet I'll take."

"Sorry I brought it up. So, what's the straight skinny on you?"

"If you must know, you'll just have to figure it out like everybody else."

"Sometimes I wonder why I put up with you, Masterson."

"Wisdom."

"Wisdom?"

"Where else could you come by it so cheap?"

CHAPTER FOURTEEN

Dodge City
August 1878

In addition to prurient pursuits, Dodge offered higher tone entertainments that summer. The Comique had Eddie Foy. Ham Bell's Varieties Theatre headlined the vocal talents of the lovely Fannie Keenan, known off stage as Dora Hand. Dora was a big hit in Dodge both for her singing and charming personality. Off stage she mingled with the upper crust of Dodge society and became an active member of the Ladies Aid.

Cowboy James "Spike" Kenedy arrived with a King Ranch herd later that summer. Kenedy was the son of a King Ranch partner, the famously wealthy Mifflin Kenedy. Born to wealth and privilege, young Spike held himself and his reckless personal conduct above the law. On July 29, Wyatt hauled the young tough into police court for violating the city ordinance against carrying firearms. Charlie Bassett followed that up with an arrest on disorderly conduct charges.

The arrogant young Kenedy felt persecuted. It was plain enough these law dogs held no proper respect for a personage of his station. He poured out his grievances to Mayor James "Dog" Kelley one evening in Kelley's Alhambra Saloon. Kelley sided with his canine cousins in law enforcement and assured Kenedy the lawmen were acting on his authority, and that, should he, Kenedy, fail to discipline his conduct, he should expect more and worse of the same brand of treatment. The hothead flew into a rage and made the mistake of assaulting what he saw as the slender, weak-jawed Kelley. Kelley mopped the floor with the upstart and unceremoniously threw him into the street, whereupon Kenedy vowed vengeance.

Kenedy left Dodge following the incident, headed for Kansas City, as we were later to learn. Dog Kelley, too, left Dodge shortly thereafter to seek medical attention at Fort Dodge. In what he expected to be a prolonged absence he rented his house behind the Western Hotel to Miss Dora Hand and another female performer from the Comique. The arrangement, convenient to all parties, proved tragic.

You wonder how reputations became distorted. September that year saw events that serve to illustrate the point. I know. I was out of town at the time. The notorious gunman Clay Allison came to Dodge looking to settle accounts with law enforcement over the death of fellow Texan George Hoy. By some accounts, the rumored bounty on Wyatt may also have entered into it.

Allison comes to town backed by twenty-five well-armed cowboys. He imbibes his way around town, one saloon after another, searching for the object of his ire. By the time he reached his last chance, he'd sufficiently imbibed to be drunk. The object of his quest, the reason for it, and the eventual outcome of his sotted search all give rise to a controversy of accounts.

By some accounts, Allison was out to kill Wyatt in revenge over Hoy's killing. By other accounts, his hunt was motivated by the bounty on Wyatt. By some accounts, Wyatt faced him down and talked him out of his purpose. By other accounts, Allison never found Wyatt. Legend aside, the latter is likely the case, as Wyatt and the rest of civil authority at the time were otherwise occupied with the threat of Dull Knife's renegade Cheyenne uprising.

That should be enough conflicted events for any one story, but it isn't. Another version of events held Allison was on the hunt for me. Why is less certain. By some accounts, I cowered in terror of the Texas gunny. By other accounts, I hid out in a second-floor room, while covering Allison's drunken pilgrimage through town behind the sights of a Sharps big fifty. By yet another account, Allison was put up to the killing of Wyatt by a prominent saloon owner in town who thought strict law enforcement bad for business. By this version of events, I accosted Allison's sponsor with a sawed-off shotgun and forced him to step between Wyatt and Allison to persuade Allison to give it up.

Such is the nature of historical record. What we do know is that Wyatt, Allison, and I figuratively walked away from the encounter none the worse for wear with our various reputations further burnished by legend.

Shanley's Grill
Forty-Third and Broadway
"You were out of town."

"I was."

"Had nothing to do with it."

"Nothing."

"And Wyatt?"

I shook my head. "Far as I know."

"How does this stuff get started?"

"A friend of Allison's named Charlie Siringo peddled some of it. Word of mouth and 'I-can-top-that' story-tellers had their way with the rest."

"I'm beginning to understand legendary reputation. I suppose there's more."

"There is."

"Tomorrow then?"

"Sure."

"Lundy's?"

I gave him my best "you've-got-to-be-kidding" look.

"OK." He slid out of the booth.

Dodge City
October 4, 1878

Spike Kenedy rode into Dodge along a deserted Front Street in the chill dead of night. He rode a dark thoroughbred race horse purchased for speed. A brace of Colt .44's slung on his hips, with a Winchester carbine tucked in his saddle boot. Thin mists of steam, pale in starlight, marked the passing of rider and horse. He disappeared north on Bridge Street.

Shots rang out in the still, small hours of night. A bartender in the lone saloon still open for business ran to his batwings in

132

time to observe a familiar lone rider gallop down the street headed west out of town.

Wyatt and his brother Jim responded to the disturbance. They found Dora Hand shot dead in Mayor Kelley's bed. Her hysterical roommate reported she'd awakened to the shots followed by the sounds of a galloping horse. Belle Dora lay in repose, a bullet through her heart fired through the wall. Given the circumstances, Wyatt and Jim suspected Spike Kenedy. Dora Hand found herself an unfortunate stead for Dog Kelley. Their suspicion was quickly confirmed by the observant bartender. Jurisdiction passed to me when the suspect left town.

I came on the scene at dawn to organize a posse. Given the young woman's popularity, we had no shortage of volunteers. I expected Kenedy would seek haven in Texas. I doubted he'd risk travel down the near end of the Great Western given his westerly departure. I expected he'd turn south for a Cimarron River ford near Wagon Bed Springs and from there proceed into Texas. With a generous head start on a fast horse, the odds stacked up for a long pursuit. Should he reach Texas, he might very well seek comfort in the armed protection of his father's many men. I needed competent posse men to take up such a challenge. City Marshal Charlie Bassett and Wyatt Earp, along with deputies Bill Duffey and Bill Tilghman, signed on.

We rode out that afternoon headed for Wagon Bed Springs by a southwesterly route, betting we could catch our man at the ford. We got off to a rough start when a hailstorm blew in. The storm prompted Wyatt to grumble about my penchant for foul weather pursuits. Ice pellets turned to cold, heavy rain. We rode on through the night. Hard men do that despite damnable discomfort. We'd hunted the region long enough to hold our line without benefit of trail sign or celestials to navigate by. We reached the ford at dawn.

A settler near the ford told us he hadn't seen anyone cross before the storm hit. It felt like we'd made good our hunch. We settled in to wait. Bill Tilghman was on watch when a lone rider appeared in the distance. He called us to alert. Wyatt put a telescope on him.

"It's him," he said.

Kenedy approached to within fifty yards or so of the ford and spotted us. He wheeled away and spurred up a gallop. We cut loose with our long guns and dropped that magnificent horse; terrible waste that was.

Pinned Kenedy under him where he fell. He took a ball in the arm that shattered the bone; took the fight out of him. For all of it, he still had vengeance in his craw, inquiring as to whether he'd killed Kelley. He shut up in some remorse on learning he'd murdered Dora Hand.

We packed him back to Dodge and locked him in the hoosegow. Doc patched him up as best he could. He lay between life and judgment for days. He faced inquest from his jail cell in the presence of Judge R. G. Cook, whereupon he was released for lack of evidence.

Shanley's Grill
Forty-Third and Broadway

"Lack of evidence? He confessed," Runyon said. "Then it must be so."

"What must be so?"

"Reports say his father showed up with enough cash to smooth over the grave."

"Rumors. Mifflin Kenedy did come to town. Took the boy to Fort Dodge for medical attention. They took his arm; he didn't last long after that. Stories varied. Some say he picked a gun scrape with a better hand back in Texas. Others say complications from his wound killed him."

"What about the money? He confessed.

How much more evidence did the judge need? It had to be money."

"Don't know anything about that."

Runyon furrowed a skeptical brow as he stubbed out a cigarette. "If it wasn't money got the kid off, then what?"

Sleeping dogs.

I glanced at my watch. "Emma will be waiting for me." I started to leave.

"Lunch?"

"The Metropole."

"Not Lundy's?"

"The Metropole."

"Noon."

"See you then."

CHAPTER FIFTEEN

Dodge City

With the cattle season over and Kenedy behind bars, things settled down to the winter routine. The denizens of Dodge City passed the time in winter gambling and drinking. The fight for warmth fueled the consumption of strong spirits, for some to excess. While we made far fewer incarcerations for intoxication than we did during the season, public drunkenness remained the leading cause of occupancy in our iron-bar hotel. We got to know the regular drunks in town. A few gave us friendly concern for their well-being. Wyatt worried over Doc. Out of friendship for Wyatt, I suggested a cure we'd plied to good effect on some.

The cure began by buying the drunk subject a drink. One led to another and more, until the subject inevitably passed out. The subject was then removed to the undertaker where he, or in one case she, was laid to rest in an open coffin. We powdered the face to a pasty white looking up into a mirror suspended from the ceiling. Thereupon concerned family, friends, and neighbors took up our vigil, feigning the appearance of a wake for the benefit of the subject's moment of awakening.

As you might imagine it made for a rude awakening. A glimpse into the impending abyss. Confronted with dissipation, more than a few sobered up. Not all, mind you, but enough to encourage the practice for those in need. We seldom attempted the cure until family or friends solicited our help. With the support of family and friends, prospects for a cure improved. It became well worth the try.

Metropole Hotel
Forty-Second and Broadway
Runyon stubbed out his cigarette. "Should have known you back when I first started fighting my demon. Might have gotten me off the sauce sooner. Did it work on Doc?"

"Never tried it. Once we thought about it, it would never have worked with Doc. It worked on those capable of reform. Doc's disposition was too jaded. Death already had a firm grip on him, drunk or sober. We weren't sure he'd even notice the pallor on his skin for the one he wore every day. Then there was the practical problem. No one had any idea how much whisky it would take for him to pass out. He drank all the time. Mostly got to a steady state of inebriation and stuck there. He knew he was dying; the reaper had him by the collar. Likely Doc found the cycle-totter more agreeable drunk than sober."

"Sad."

"It was and it wasn't. The disease was sad. I didn't like the man much, but I'll give him this: he went his own way. Takes a man to do that when he's dealt the queen of spades."

"What's next?"

"Let's see . . . 1879; that'd pretty soon bring us to the Royal Gorge war, though we had a little lawing to do before we got there."

Dodge City
Spring 1879

Spring began to warm and bud. The cattle drive season hadn't started yet, but we had visitors to Dodge passing through. Wyatt was making his rounds one night when a ruckus broke out in the Long Branch. The rowdies were three Missouri men with belligerence left over from the war. The leader was a big, raw-boned loudmouth Wyatt sized up from the batwings. He waved me in from up the street to back up what looked to be a routine buffaloing. I stepped into the shadows where I could keep an eye on things while Wyatt entered the saloon.

Wyatt collared the leader, informing him he'd had enough, and that he'd be a guest of the city for the rest of the night. Wyatt hustled the man out the door and headed down the street toward the jail. The other two looked at each other and followed them out the door.

I sensed there might be trouble and followed along. The pair drew concealed guns and ordered Wyatt to release their pal. The leader made a play for Wyatt's gun, for which he received the buffaloing he deserved. I stepped in, guns drawn, and disarmed the other two. We hauled the lot of them off to the hoosegow. All in a seven-dollar-and-fifty-cents night's work.

In the morning the boys from Missouri paid their fines and left town, or so we thought. Unbeknownst to us, the Missourians doubled back to town at dusk. They set up shop at the back of the alley beside the Western Hotel, leading to the Kelley cabin where Dora Hand had met her demise. They paid a young lad to summon the sheriff to a fictitious altercation. Smart lad thought it odd — three men and no sign of trouble. The boy summoned me all right, but not without a warning something didn't seem right. His description of the men put the finger on the Missouri men. I doubled his tip by way of thanks and summoned Bill Tilghman and my brother Jim.

Bill and Jim circled around behind the hotel while I presented myself at the mouth of the alley. All appeared quiet. My attention riveted on a window to a storeroom at the back of the building across the alley from the hotel. I stopped short of a shooting angle and waited.

Time passed. The Missourians were left to suspect I hadn't taken the bait. Tilghman appeared in the moonlight at the back of the alley. I pointed to the storeroom. Bill and Jim took up positions on either side of the building's back door. When the Missouri men grew tired of their fruitless wait, we collared the lot for the second time. Breaking and entering the charge this time. We hauled them off to the iron-bar hotel. The next morning the fines were heavy enough to induce the trio to shake their boots of Dodge dust for good.

Later That Spring

The engine of commerce drove westward expansion. Fur trade, railroads, buffalo hides, beef — you name it. Markets and profits propelled wagons and rails West. Through all those years booms followed gold and silver. And so it came to pass a silver strike near Leadville, Colorado, set in motion the greatest rail race since the Union Pacific and Central Pacific amassed right-of-way empires along with their tracks.

Railroads learned the value of freight on buffalo hides and later beef. Silver shipping out of Colorado made for a shiny prize, a prize that would belong to the line that controlled track through the Royal Gorge. The Leadville boom pitted the Atchison, Topeka, & Santa Fe against the Denver & Rio Grande. Right of way through the Colorado Royal Gorge became hotly contested. The gorge was a narrow defile, scarcely wide enough for a single rail bed. Carved over millennia by the Arkansas River, the gorge passed between thousand-foot shear heights covering a span not quite a quarter mile in length. Engineering made it one dearly expensive section of track. Nature made it a deadly construction challenge. Silver made it a prize worthy of the price.

Both companies were determined to control right of way through the gorge. Nominally the debt-strapped Denver & Rio Grande controlled the gorge right of way. D&RG creditors refused to finance President W. J. Palmer's request for funds to develop the section. The creditors insisted D&RG lease the right of way to the AT&SF as a source of funds to repay the line's debt. Left with no choice, Palmer reluctantly agreed. Santa Fe General Manager W. B. Strong seized the opportunity. Palmer began looking for reasons to break the lease almost before ink dried on the signatures. Track-laying crews raced toward the gorge. Armed gangs were dispatched to secure the safety of the crews and assert physical control of the gorge. Despite winning the race to the gorge, the competition strapped the financially weaker Denver & Rio Grande. Strong immediately ordered his AT&SF crews to begin the perilous task of traversing the gorge.

March 1879

Palmer chafed at the fiscal handcuffs imposed on him by his bondholders. He couldn't abide the notion of being bested by his rival. He reasoned that his board, stockholders, and investors could be brought around if he were able to reclaim rights to the gorge passage. The silver contracts were far too lucrative to pass up. He'd find a way to finance the track, but first he had to reclaim his right of way.

He filed suit in court asserting the Santa Fe had violated the terms of its lease and sought to have the agreement set aside. While the courts deliberated the merits of his claim, he dispatched armed men to fortify positions above the gorge in an effort to stop the AT&SF from further developing the right of way until such time as his claim might be adjudicated.

Whereupon Santa Fe officials at Canon City requested that I, in my capacity as deputy U.S. marshal — a position I had accepted earlier that year — recruit a posse, financed by the railroad, to enforce the Santa Fe's claim. Competent men were quickly drawn to the cause by the promise of light duty, good pay and found.

We decamped to the gorge at Canon City in company of some thirty men, including such notables as Ben Thompson, Doc Holliday, and Josh Webb. We found the gorge well fortified by stone emplacements on the heights defended by some fifty men. A stalemate ensued, punctuated occasionally by ineffectual gunfire I quickly quelled in my capacity as peace officer. Such skirmishes inflicted no harm on either side.

The stalemate remained joined until April 21st, when a court of competent jurisdiction ruled the Denver & Rio Grande held first claim on the Royal Gorge right of way. My men and I returned to Dodge, thinking the matter settled.

June 1879

Meanwhile, back in Canon City, AT&SF General Manager Strong commenced fortifying his stations for defense until such time as his appeals might be satisfied. I received a request to once again raise a posse to participate in defense of the AT&SF's stations. Some sixty men were soon rallied to my call to secure AT&SF's bases of operation, including the depot and roundhouse at Pueblo Colorado, which was given to my personal safekeeping.

The roundhouse at Pueblo offered services essential to operation of a railroad and a fortress-like structure suited to our defensive purposes. Notable friends in our number included Mysterious Dave Mather and Dave Rudabaugh, in addition to the aforementioned Ben Thompson and Doc Holliday. Mystery surrounded Mather's activities, likely for their having crossed the lines of legality in company with Rudabaugh. As his sobriquet implied, he remained cloaked in a veil of mystery for lack of arrests and convictions. By contrast, there was no mystery concerning the lethality of his pistols. Battle lines were hastily drawn for the conflict to come.

June 10, 1879
Judicial district court in Alamosa ordered the Santa Fe to turn over its Denver & Rio Grande leasehold. The court order instructed sheriffs in the affected areas to oversee return of Denver & Rio Grande property. Thus, in the stroke of its order, the court pitted legal jurisdictions against one another in support of parties on both sides of the dispute.

It turned out Strong wasn't the only one anticipating the judge's decision. Palmer had his ear on the telegraph lines to Colorado Springs. He learned of Strong's plan to resist the court order, expecting it to be reversed on appeal. He instructed his men all along the line to call on local sheriffs to move immediately to enforce the court order. At six o'clock on the morning of June 11, sheriffs backed by Denver & Rio Grande gunmen served the court's order on all Santa Fe men stationed along the line.

Some fighting took place in West Denver and Colorado Springs, but resistance was short lived.

In Pueblo, we knew none of this. Denver & Rio Grande forces quickly took the depot and water tank. We let them have both. We'd make our stand in the roundhouse. The sheriff and his mercenary posse didn't know it, but we'd seen fit to borrow a six-pound howitzer, shot, and powder stored at a nearby state armory and deployed it in defense of the roundhouse.

Realization the sheriff's posse faced opposition defended by primed artillery occasioned request for a parley. It was then I learned the rest of the line had been taken, leaving us the last holdout. The court's order had yet to be reversed, the certainty of which depended on which side you spoke to. Not wanting to be the cause of bloodshed under the circumstances, we agreed to surrender the roundhouse and return to Dodge.

Metropole Hotel
Forty-Second and Broadway
I dabbed the last bit of Waldorf salad from my chin with a napkin. The Metropole menu didn't admit their rival's recipe had made it to their selection of lunch fare, not

in so many words, but I knew. Runyon popped the last bite of watercress on wheat in his mouth, tapped a cigarette from its package, and lit up. No doubt his intention to rid his palate of the aftertaste of that dreadful sandwich. No wonder he favored that deli.

"Watercress. I swear, Runyon, you've the tastebuds of a rabbit."

"A sophisticated rabbit."

"How sophisticated can a rabbit be?"

"Sophisticated enough to appreciate good watercress."

"There's no such thing as good watercress."

"How would you know? Let's get back to what you do know. So there ended the Royal Gorge war."

"It did."

"Would you have used the cannon?"

"If the need had arisen."

"That would have written yet another chapter in Bat Masterson's notoriety."

"Likely so."

"Surrender seems unlike you."

"I suppose it does. Doc and Ben said as much at the time. We held a strong position. The roundhouse could only have been taken at fearsome cost — death to those who might attempt an assault and destruction, should the opposition have resorted to dynamite."

"I hadn't thought of explosives."

"I did, though I was confident they'd not resort to that. Losing the roundhouse would have rendered the line useless to either side until it could be rebuilt. Explosives would have been a poor business decision. In that case, money proved the better barricade."

"So, in the end, the courts decided for the Denver & Rio Grande, and the Santa Fe lost."

"For a time. The silver ran out before the Denver & Rio Grande took a return on their investment in bridging the gorge. I suspect Palmer's subsequent financial pain afforded Strong something of a last laugh. I couldn't indulge myself in such at the time; I had my own troubles back in Dodge."

"Oh?"

"Politics. Reelection politics." I glanced at my watch. "That will have to wait. I'm on deadline."

"At least these deadlines aren't injurious to your health."

"There is that."

"Shanley's for dinner tomorrow?"

CHAPTER SIXTEEN

Dodge City
September 1879

Life took a new turn that fall, though I didn't see it coming at the time. Early in September, Wyatt came by the office. He told me he planned to resign his city marshal's appointment and pull up stakes for Arizona. He was tired of the law dog business and the hazards of a gun hand profession. His brothers were cashing in on a silver strike around Tombstone. He asked if I cared to join him. I told him I was obliged to serve out the balance of my current term as sheriff and planned to stand for reelection to a second two-year term later that fall.

Wyatt had no more than boarded the train west when trouble began brewing around my reelection. Throughout my term as sheriff, I'd enjoyed good relations with community leaders some folks called the Dodge

City Gang. These businessmen, led by Bob Wright, wielded considerable political influence from the mayor's office and city council. As their businesses concentrated on mercantile and sporting diversions catering to the end-of-trail cowboy clientele, they favored my brand of law, which allowed sport in good fun, so long as public safety was assured.

Dodge had prospered and grown in those trail's-end years. Growth brought a more genteel aspect to society, one that favored a more strictly enforced brand of decorum. I hadn't noticed. Content with the diligent performance of my duties and the unwavering approval of my supporters, my political future seemed assured.

Opposition to my candidacy asserted itself in a series of unflattering newspaper editorials accusing me of various and spurious offenses, including dereliction of duty, fraud, and corruption. The culprits were a pair of unscrupulous purveyors of foul smelling yellow-dog editorialism. The principal culprit was Bob Fry, editor of the *Speareville News,* Speareville being a nondescript crosshatching of ruts at the east end of the county. Left to its own, Fry's little rag wouldn't have amounted to much damage, but such was not to be the case. Dan Frost of the *Ford County Globe* played echo to Fry's fables.

I was furious. The allegations were slanderous and baseless. I vowed to raise the most strenuous of objections. My politically astute friends and advisors, Mike Sutton and Nick Klaine, editor of the *Dodge City Times,* cautioned against "dignifying the accusations with a response." People knew me, they argued. No one would believe such nonsense. I acquiesced to their seemingly sagacious advice. Klaine came to my defense in the *Times,* dismissing his rivals' assertions. Newspaper editorials, after all, represented nothing more than opinion. None of the claimed falsehoods were borne out in fact. No one brought charges, let alone any proceeding that might result in a verdict. Those who knew me could not be deceived.

I was about to learn a bitter lesson with respect to the power of the pen, even a pen dipped in the poisonous ink of falsehood, when coupled with the insidious influence the reform-minded might wield. It was my first encounter with the morally self-righteous reformer engaged in a battle against individual freedoms and liberties that follows me to this very day.

My erstwhile advisors had been right on one point: those who knew me were indeed not deceived. The fact overlooked was that Dodge had grown. Prosperity came with the cattle trade. Prosperity bred growth. Those who did not know me, the more pious and genteel newcomers to Dodge, read the editorials and heard the evils of demon rum, gambling, and sporting doves denounced from the pulpit on an idyllic Sunday morn. Those good souls were deceived, and they voted my opponent, George Hinkle, into office.

I am, I confess, a graceless loser. Stinging humiliation does not wear well on me. My loyal supporters and advisors expressed due sympathy on their way to curry favor with the new sheriff. Politics, I learned, makes for strange bedfellows. So does prostitution. Both indulge in temporary satisfactions for money.

And so the whims of political fortune threw me to the gutter like yesterday's table scraps. Innuendo, rumor, and baseless allegations put forth by a hostile and thoroughly dishonest press did me untold damage. This afforded me my first bitter taste of the bucolic churl spewed by moralistic cretins in the name of reform. Slander identified me with supposed abuses of civility and social order the duties of my office were charged to protect, defend, and uphold.

True, I'd gotten bad advice in regard to ignoring the smears. I'd compounded that on my own behalf by accepting it. The part that stuck sideways in my craw in a fashion I shall never forget is the fact that, in the court of public opinion, the charge is all that matters. Guilt or innocence, truth or falsehood need not enter into consideration. My natural inclinations to distrust the reform minded hardened on that bitter lesson.

The winter of 1880 forced me to take stock of my station. Much had changed on the frontier since my arrival. Commercial buffalo hunting had for all practical purposes come to an end. Some made a business in gathering bones, but I had no stomach for it, or hip, for that matter. Indians had largely been settled to reservations. Indian fighters and army scouts were no longer in demand. Civilization had come to the boom towns and cow towns. They had no need for peace officers whose gun reputations preserved law and order. It seemed all the skills I'd amassed to this point in my young life were of no further use to my personal prosperity. I did find one bright spot in the cracked mirror of my life, one skill that might yet profitably amuse me. Owing to the idle evenings of many a buffalo camp, I'd become a fair hand as a gambler. Reputation preceded me into the gambling dens of the West, where owners and operators concerned for security found comfort in my presence should I serve in their employ. My prospects drifted toward a livelihood at the tables of chance.

Leadville, Colorado Territory
January 1880

Reflection led me to Leadville, Colorado, with its high-stakes games played at silver-enriched tables. Leadville had a game for every taste, talent, and appetite for risk. Faro was my game of choice. I could play for the house or buck the tiger for my own account. You could take your choice of venue, from Kitty's game at the California Concert Hall to the Board of Trade or Texas House. Respectable names, respectable games. Gambling in those days was considered something of an honorable endeavor for those who played square. With my reputation for honest play and a gun able to back up my game, I found myself in demand. I could command a handsome salary dealing for the house, with my reputation keeping a lid on the losers. I could have, but I didn't. Bucking the tiger suited my appetite for excitement and profit in my purse.

I passed the winter in Leadville on a good run at the tables. I got the notion I could make a living as a gambler. It made for an easier life than that of a law man. No more long rides through bitter winters or scorching summers chasing some scoundrel who might be lying in wait around the next bend in the trail aiming to put a bullet in you. No more skull-busting drunken cowboys too full of liquid courage to judge the trouble they were in. Not that gambling came without risk; sore losers could be a problem. Gamblers played where drunks hung out, but the sporting life offered two advantages where trouble was concerned. The sober were cowed by my reputation. I could buffalo a sore loser with a scowl or a little evil eye. If a drunk became disorderly, it wasn't my problem, unless he threatened my life. I didn't find much concern in that. All things considered, the sporting life suited me.

I salted away enough money that winter to establish my own gambling house. When that possibility arose, I ruminated over where to locate it. I don't consider myself a spiteful person. Vengeance, as they say, is a dish best served cold. Still, I do have a memory. My thoughts wandered toward Dodge. The idea of opening a sporting parlor under the very upturned noses of my political adversaries gave off a sweet aroma. The fact that it might compete with some of my former supporters added a dash of spice to the notion of sampling a taste.

Spurred on by my own indulgence, I returned to Dodge that spring when the streets surrendered their frost to mud ruts. While reflecting on opportunities to invest my newfound wealth in an establishment suited to my purposes, an old friend tugged at my sleeve.

CHAPTER SEVENTEEN

Dodge City
March 1880

Ben Thompson had a problem, or, more to the point, his brother Billy had a problem. No surprise that. I had not much use for Billy Thompson. He had a knack for getting into troubles he couldn't manage his way through. Brother Ben, it seemed, was always there to bail him out, though, in this case, therein lay Ben's problem.

Billy got himself in a shooting scrape on the wrong side of the law in Ogallala, Nebraska. He was wounded, in custody, and a subject of interest to angry locals who favored hanging bee justice over due process by the blind lady. Ben, having previously worn out his welcome in Ogallala, prevailed on me to go to his brother's aid. As I say, I wasn't much inclined to do it for the no-account Billy, but Ben had backed my play with Corporal King in the Lady Gay incident and signed on to my part in the Royal Gorge affair. I figured I owed him, troublesome brother or no. Bat Masterson abides his debts, and so it was I entrained for Nebraska.

Ogallala, Nebraska

I stepped off the train at a wide spot in the prairie north of the Union Pacific tracks. Kansas is known for its gusty, strong prairie winds. While our fair territory may enjoy the reputation, the good people of Nebraska have the pleasure of living up to it. A brief enquiry at the sheriff's office, posing as Billy's attorney, informed me he was being held at the hotel, owing to his injuries. Approaching the hotel, I counted the circumstances both good news and bad. For good news, I wouldn't have to break him out of Ogallala's two-cell jail. The other side of that fortune was the cracker-box hotel would afford precious little resistance, should local vigilantes elect to take Billy's fate into their own designs. Then again that risk might finish second to the risk prairie wind might blow the rickety structure down around the very ears of him I felt bound to liberate. I found Billy, complete with ten-gauge shotgun souvenirs, flat on his back in a dingy little hotel room under twenty-four

159

hour guard by a sheriff's deputy. I recalled our exchange.

"Nice place," I said.

"Nice to see you, too, Bat."

"Ben sent me."

"Thought as much."

"He here all the time?" I tossed my head at the guarded door.

Billy nodded.

I lowered my voice. "You make a slow recovery. Make it worse than it is, 'til I can figure a way out of this flea trap."

He nodded again.

I engaged the fresh-faced guard on the way out.

"Shot up as bad as he is, it's hardly worth your time to guard him."

"Sheriff's orders. No exceptions. What do you want with him?"

"Family attorney. Actually, he owes me money. I'll be back by and by to see if I can collect."

The kid laughed.

I left. The situation wasn't funny. Billy couldn't ride. Put him in a wagon, and a blind man could follow our trail in the dark. The sheriff was sighted as good as you or me; we wouldn't get very far. That left the train. Getting him on was problem one. Where to? Problem two.

I took a room in the hotel, figuring to stay close to the situation should the locals make trouble. The saloon next door served a passable steak. I took a bottle of the house finest to a table near the front window. This afforded the opportunity to watch the sun go down, while the whiskey removed any cracked or chipped paint from my inwards. After examining all the options I could drum up, I came to what might be a long shot, but at least it was a shot.

Fifty miles east of Ogallala, the U.P. stopped at North Platte. Bill Cody had a home there in those days. I'd met Cody on a buffalo hunt years back. I thought he might remember me. Maybe he'd be willing to give me a hand. It was worth a ride to North Platte to find out.

North Platte

Bill had a fine home on the outskirts of town. Jovial as ever, he remembered the twenty-year-old kid I'd been on the occasion of our first meeting. He knew my name from my sheriff days in Dodge. I helped him put the two together.

"So, what brings you to North Platte, Bat? I can't think it's old times."

"No," I shook my head. "Ben Thompson's kid brother got himself in a law scrape over in Ogallala. Ben's a good friend. He asked me to help get his brother out from under a hangman's noose."

"Ben Thompson . . . I know that name, too. Brotherly concern; where do I come in?"

"The kid is shot up. He can't ride. The only way to get him out and away is the train. I need to get him back to Dodge. I figure if I can get him on the train as far as North Platte, we can make it the rest of the way by wagon."

"No need to ask more. I'll have a carriage waiting when you get here."

"Mighty generous of you, Bill."

"You just tell Ben I pitched in."

"Consider it done."

Ogallala, Nebraska

Back in Ogallala we caught a break. Two breaks really. I stopped in at Billy's hotel room to check on him. On my way out, still puzzling over how to get him out, I stopped by the hotel bar for a drink. There I was greeted by a familiar face with a friendly grin. The bartender had worked in Dodge. Jim something . . . I don't recall for sure. He asked me what I was doing in Ogallala. I explained I was looking after Billy Thompson.

"Looking to spring him," he said.

No point lying over the obvious. I nodded. "Got to figure a way to get him out of here before the locals fit him for a necktie."

The red-haired kid got a mischievous glint in them green eyes of his. He must have been Irish now that I think about it. Anyway, he leans over the bar and whispers. I slapped the bar with a good laugh and ordered us both a drink.

A few days later, the rest of the riddle unraveled. I wired Cody to expect a package delivery on the Monday morning eastbound. That Sunday night, the town held a shindig up at the schoolhouse. Everyone in town went to the dance, including the sheriff, who played the fiddle. The only two exceptions, other than Billy and me, were Jim and the hapless deputy left on guard duty. I went up to Billy's room, checked on him, and sympathized with the deputy over the misery of his having to miss the party. Overflowing with the goodness of my heart, I offered to buy him a drink and hollered downstairs for Jim to bring us a couple whiskies with lemon. He brought up the first. I sent him back for a second. Twenty minutes later, our stalwart young deputy lay stretched out, snoring at peace with the angels. You can't get lemons like that just anywhere.

I got Billy downstairs and across the street under cover of darkness to the depot platform just as the eastbound rolled in. I helped him into the Pullman to the fiddle strains of a reel wafting over the evening breeze. A few minutes later, we rolled out of town.

North Platte
Monday Morning
Bill Cody met us at the station in a cabriolet pulled by a finely matched bay harness pair. We loaded Billy up and drove off to Cody's place. We laid low for a week with our ears to the ground for news out of Ogallala. Word went out Billy Thompson was on the loose, but, when no one reported seeing him, the trail went cold pretty fast. The following week we accompanied Cody and a party of well-to-do hunters from the East out for a taste of the West as far south as their ranch destination. There we bid our adieus with much appreciation to our host and set out by wagon for Dodge. Far from the luxury of the carriage, it was a horrible trip. Two hundred miles through cold spring rain. For all the misery, we made it to Dodge, much to Ben Thompson's relief, gratitude, and the satisfaction of my debt.

"That was a good steak." Runyon wiped his lips on a napkin and tapped a cigarette out of the packet. "Better than the fare in that Ogallala saloon I'll wager."

I remembered. "It is, though dust adds a certain gritty character to a meal one overlooks when hungry enough."

"And you grouse about Lundy's."

"Grit I can swallow. Bustle and noise disturb digestive tranquility."

Runyon exhaled a cloud of smoke under an uplifted brow. "A man of your reputed skill and courage has a tender stomach. I find that hard to believe."

"Tender? No. I merely have my preferences."

"Preferences. Prejudices, you mean."

"I don't prefer your deli atmosphere."

"It's New York."

"So you say."

"We've had this conversation. So, did you open a gambling parlor?"

"My plans changed before I found the right property."

"How so?"

"A letter from Wyatt."

CHAPTER EIGHTEEN

Dodge
1881

Things don't always turn out the way you have it figured. I should have learned that from my electoral experience as sheriff. Still, I was surprised when I received a letter from Wyatt, informing me he was back to packing a star in Tombstone. He also held an owner's share in a gambling hall called the Oriental Saloon. Silver strike stakes made gambling lucrative, but the competition was fierce, and he had his hands full with two demanding jobs. As his brothers were otherwise gainfully employed, he'd written to me and Luke Short with offers of dealing jobs in the Oriental. I found out later the competition he referred to was known to play rough at times, and the facts of Luke's and my reputations would serve to help keep a lid on things. Not being wedded to Kansas for reasons of gainful employment at the time, I decided to take him up on the offer.

I boarded a westbound train to Trinidad, Colorado, and south from there to the end of AT&SF track. The dangerous part of the trip took the overland stage from end of track through Apache country to Deming, New Mexico. Fortunately, that leg proved uneventful. I caught the Southern Pacific at Deming west to Benson, Arizona, and there boarded a southbound stage for Tombstone.

Stage travel is an expedient alternative to mounted travel where horses have to be rested, but it is seldom a pleasant alternative to a ride through open country. The Arizona desert is inhospitable under most circumstances, even less so by stage. The sun beats crucible hot out of cloudless skies. Dust boils up around a stage in a perpetual dun fog. Wind driven, it becomes stinging sand — a grit to teeth not covered by a bandanna and a crust to the reddened eye. I rode up top, exposed to the sun, but relieved of much of the dust discomfort of those confined to the coach. It also afforded engagement away from the monotony of the swaying, jolting coach.

Bob Paul, the Wells Fargo messenger on the run south from Benson, was both talkative and well acquainted with the Earps and the situation in Tombstone. He filled me in as we rode. The Earps had once again found their way into law enforcement, with Virgil acting as Tombstone city marshal and deputy U.S. marshal, while Wyatt served as Pima County deputy sheriff. These appointments put them at odds with an outlaw faction engaged in rustling, robbery, and all manner of ruthless depredations.

The Cowboys, as they were known, included the Clanton and McLaury clans, along with notable desperados Johnny Ringo, Frank Stillwell, Billy Clairborne, Curly Bill Brocius, and Pony Deal. Wyatt and Virgil could count on brother Morgan and Doc Holliday for competent allies. Outnumbered should festivities boil over, the Earps received support from the law-abiding business community, while the Cowboys operated with impunity under the sympathetic nose of neighboring Cochise County sheriff, Johnny Behan. If all this weren't bad enough, Wyatt had personal enmity with Behan over the favors of a woman. Ah, the fair sex. An incendiary ingredient where tensions arouse among men. My hip afforded constant reminder. The situation Bob Paul described had all the ingredients for large scale trouble. I felt myself being drawn into far more than dealing a game of faro. I might have decided there were far less risky employment opportunities to be had, had it not been for my friendship with Wyatt. If he'd written me all the sordid details and asked my help, I'd have undertaken the journey, employment offer notwithstanding. Friends do that. Wyatt, I knew, would have done as much for me.

Tombstone

I took stock of my new surroundings as the stage rolled into town. Tombstone sprawled south and east of the mines responsible for its boom existence. The central avenue ran east and west along Allen Street, between Third and Sixth Streets. The architecture favored adobe, a building material in ample supply, with timber and frame reserved for higher purposes such as shading walkways. I found Wyatt's Oriental Saloon on the north side of Allen at Fifth. By reference that placed it a block south of Fremont and two blocks east of the O.K. Corral, destined to become more significant later that year.

On reaching the Oriental I was pleased to find Luke Short there to make something more of evening the odds I'd learned from Bob Paul on the ride down from Benson. We undertook our dealing appointments in the Oriental. Wyatt had himself a fine establishment there by the rough standards of a mining camp gambling hall. It was much the sort of establishment I might have purchased had I found such a property back in Dodge. Wyatt had fairly stated the appetite for higher stakes gaming. As Luke and I settled in to our new positions, we soon learned the Oriental would provide the opportunity of a fine living.

It didn't take long for word of our arrival to spread. Soon enough elements of the Clanton and McLaury cowboy factions made appearances to check on the cut of our reputations. I might not have recognized these visits at first. Wyatt would point them out while checking on the games. Virgil, too, identified a couple of them while making his rounds. It didn't take long before I could feel the attention when one of them dropped in to give us the once-over. It's not that I minded being measured like that; it gave Luke and me a chance to see what we might be up against. None of them looked too threatening by my lights. We'd all faced their kind and worse, keeping a lid on Dodge. I gathered the Cowboys had not much interest in us. Their complaints were with Wyatt and Virgil. We were of interest only so far as we might be seen backing our friends' play. Over all, I think our presence served to slake their appetite for confrontation, if not the tensions giving rise to it. We made a formidable lot when you added the likes of Doc, Luke, and me to the Earps. That's surely where things stood following the Storms affair.

Soon after taking up our employ at the Oriental, I arrived one morning to find Luke finishing a long night dealing faro with a disgruntled loser on his hands. Charlie Storms was a well-known high-stakes player and a man with whom I was well acquainted and on friendly terms. I sensed the dispute about to go to gun play and stepped between the belligerents.

"Don't shoot," I said to Luke, turning my attention to Charlie.

"Come along, my friend. Let's step outside for a breath of fresh air before matters here become unpleasant."

"What business is this of yours, Masterson?"

"A business to see to it neither of my friends gets hurt. Now come along."

I urged him by the elbow of his gun hand. He relented and followed along.

Outside, I hoped the cool morning air would have a sobering effect on Charlie. He may have had an impulse to go for his gun with Short. Luke's small stature often invited his adversaries to underestimate him. Such misjudgment could prove an error I doubted Charlie Storms would survive.

"Have you been at it all night?"

He nodded.

"Let's get you to your bed then. You could use some sleep. Things will likely look better after a little shuteye."

We went along to his room and tucked him away. I thought the matter settled and returned to the Oriental, where Luke was wrapping up his shift.

"I was perfectly capable of handling him," he said.

"I know. He wasn't capable of handling you. He just didn't know that."

"So you explained his troubles to him?"

"Of course not. I put him to bed. Charlie Storms is all right. Given the chance I should think the two of you might find friendly terms."

"I'm the prince of pleasantry with those who mind their manners."

I laughed at the thought of a princely Luke Short and accompanied him out to the boardwalk. We'd no more than cleared the batwings when Luke was set upon by the person of Charlie Storms, who jerked him off the boardwalk into the street brandishing a short-barrel Colt in his hand. Luke was quick. His pistol appeared at Storms's heart and charged, muzzle flash flaring his shirt. Storms fell to a finishing round, dead before he hit the ground.

It didn't take long for word of Storms's fate to spread. That Luke bested a man, gun in hand, with his draw became a matter of no small curiosity about town. It prompted a new round of Cowboy visits to the Oriental. Some of them, it would appear, came to mistrust their earlier estimations where we were concerned. Reputations of past acts, it seems, were not only validated; I suspect they were embellished by the sensation of eye-witness accounts.

CHAPTER NINETEEN

March 15

Wyatt entered the Oriental early one evening. The tables were quiet, awaiting the late crowd. I could tell something was amiss by the grim set to his jaw and the purpose to his stride. He motioned me to the bar.

"Trouble?" I asked.

"Got a wire from Bob Paul. Road agents hit the Benson stage near Drew Ranch."

"They get anything?"

"Bob saved the shipment, eighty thousand in silver. They killed the driver and a passenger. Get your trail gear and meet me at the office. I'll swear you in there. We're goin' after 'em."

"What about the game?"

"Luke's got it. Let's move."

I arrived at the office a short time later to find Virgil, Morgan, and the Wells Fargo agent. Wyatt swore us in. We mounted up and rode north on a clear starlit night.

174

Around midnight I jogged along stirrup to stirrup with Wyatt.

"Any idea who did it?"

Wyatt lifted the white of one eye under his hat brim. "Cowboys is my wager. Bob thought he recognized one of 'em for a man known to ride for the Clantons."

We reached Drew Ranch shortly before dawn. Bob Paul was there to meet us. Curiously, we found Sheriff Behan and his deputy there, having previously arrived. Bob wired Wyatt; Behan's presence seemed unexplained. He and Wyatt eyed each other like two roosters circling the same henhouse. I knew something of the background on Behan courtesy of Bob Paul. This would be my firsthand look at the man who would play a part in later events for both Wyatt and me.

"What are you doing here?" Wyatt asked.

"I might ask the same of you," Behan said.

"My jurisdiction. Bob here sent for me."

"I got word, too."

"From who?"

"Not important."

"You say not important; maybe it is. Maybe your information came from someone with first-hand knowledge of the incident."

"All I know is what Bob here told me.

Three gunmen threw down on the coach in order to stop it. The driver slapped his horses into a gallop. Paul got one load of shot off before the driver was hit and he was forced to take the reins. The passenger, riding up top, was killed as the coach drove away."

"That true, Bob?"

"That's what I said as far as he goes."

"You got something more?"

"Pretty sure two of the men were Clanton men."

"Missed that tidbit, did we, Johnny?"

"Speculation. I deal in facts."

"So do I. Including facts that smell."

We searched the area and found cartridge casings and sign where a fourth man held their horses in hiding. I thought it odd, given the size of the prize, that they made no attempt to overtake the coach. They had a near defenseless driver outnumbered with a team panting for relief at the next station. Instead, trail sign fled east toward the mountains.

"Mount up," Wyatt said. "Trail sign's plain enough."

Behan spit. "You goin' after 'em, Earp? Them outlaws got more'n a half-day's head start."

"You give up on all your pursuits after a

half day, Johnny? Or just when you pursue your pals?"

"What's that s'posed to mean?"

"Oh, that's right. My mistake. You'll hang on a cold trail if there's a woman involved."

"Why you . . . I've a good mind to . . ."

"No, you don't. If you did, you'd do your job. But then you'd run the risk of catching your friends red handed. Couldn't have that now, could we?"

"One of these days your loose talk is gonna catch up with you, Earp, and when it does . . ."

"Maybe so, Johnny boy, but it'd take more man than you to do anything about it."

Wyatt swung into the saddle and rode off on the trail, leaving a sputtering John Behan and a posse scrambling to catch up. Behan and his deputy trailed along, either shamed into action or more likely determined to look out for their Cowboy cronies.

We had some tracking skill among us; my experiences at buffalo hunting and Indian campaigning accounted for some of it. We managed to hang on to the trail through the night in part by skill, a well calculated hunch or two, and, no doubt, a measure of support from the fickle finger of fortune.

March 19

The third day out, we tracked one of the suspects to a ranch known to be friendly to the Cowboys. We took a man named King into custody without incident. He first claimed ignorance of the whole affair but later admitted to holding the horses and identified the other three, whose names meant nothing to me and whom I cannot now recall. At this point Behan asserted his jurisdiction, took custody of the prisoner, and returned to Cochise County. Wyatt resumed our search for the other three, which ended in futility.

The Benson stage hold-up attempt added to the bad blood brewing between the Earp brothers and the Clanton-McLaury faction. The fact the prisoner, King, promptly escaped Behan's custody only served to aggravate Wyatt's frustrations with his rival. The whole cauldron would boil over later that fall in the notorious gunfight near the O.K. Corral. That fight was to take place without me, as I was soon summoned to pressing matters of my own. I shall leave the telling of that story to those who were there. Anything I might have to say on the subject would be hearsay — those watery accounts we have in abundance with no reasonable way to sort fact from fancy.

Newspaper accounts were so divided by which side the editor favored as to be unencumbered by veracity. By some accounts the Earp brothers took down the Clanton and McLaury faction in a courageous act of law enforcement. By others, the Cowboys were cut down in cold-blooded fashion while peaceably minding their own business. A formal inquest ruled otherwise, exonerating the Earp brothers. That might have put an end to the feud, but such was not to be the case. More bloodshed was in the offing, bloodshed that would draw me into the after effects.

Shanley's Grill
Forty-Third and Broadway
I paused and glanced at my watch, thinking it getting late.

"So, there was some truth to how you and your friends got those inflated reputations."

"Only the deserved parts."

"Deserved parts?"

"There's a difference between truth and reputation. Truth is what happened; that's deserved. Reputation comes from the stuff they write to sell newspapers, magazines, and books. I never did most of the stuff that made my reputation."

"So you've said. If it bothers you, why did

you never set the record straight? You had a pen even back then. You weren't above using it, either."

"Set the record straight? Never. Reputation comes in handy when you're a professional gambler or a lawman. Men are buffaloed more by what they believe you can do than by what you actually do to them."

"So, how much should a feller believe?"

"How much does a feller want to believe?"

Finally, a little silence.

"Can I believe what you tell me?"

"Most of it; but remember, I'm old. Some things I might remember better than they actually were."

Another rest. I signaled the waiter for a check.

"Unlike you to leave Wyatt to deal with that dustup at the O.K. Corral."

"I wouldn't have if I hadn't had problems of my own."

"What sort of problem?"

"Brother Jim. See you tomorrow."

Metropole Hotel
Forty-Second and Broadway
You could feel autumn in the air when I arrived at the Metropole after work. The five o'clock crowd filed in along the bar. I grabbed our usual booth and ordered a

Manhattan. Cooler weather bespoke a warmer libation than my warm weather Tom Collins. Runyon would be along as the spirit moved him. I watched the crowd build, keeping to myself. Familiar faces in familiar places; New York, for all its size, was truly a collection of neighborhoods. Jolly Knights of the Metropole Roundtable, as the regulars were known, could be found to gather here at the close of each day's labors — labors not taken in the conventional sense. Actors, reporters, gamblers, the occasional gangster, even a baseball or football player or two, though I never craved the society of the latter.

Runyon appeared in the crowd at the door, bending the ear of ace NYPD detective Val O'Farrell, no doubt over some juicy tidbit "heard on the street." They parted with a knowing nod. I lit a cigar as Runyon made his way over to the booth. He slid in, signaling the waiter for his usual cup of coffee.

"You should choose your friends more carefully, lest you sully your reputation with the criminal elements of the city," I said.

"Oh, Val? He's all right."

"I shouldn't think so, given his considerable reputation."

"My friends know I wouldn't give him

anything good."

"You run the risk they might become confused in the matter."

"Little chance of that."

His coffee arrived.

"How so?"

"Lead poisoning."

"You're sure."

"Quite sure. You see, they know I'm quite sure." He blew on his coffee, took a sip, and tapped out a fresh cigarette. "My friends know me just as I'm sure your friends knew you. Undoubtedly, Wyatt could have counted on you when that trouble at the O.K Corral boiled up."

"He could have, though that wasn't to be."

"What happened?"

I gazed into a cloud of blue smoke.

CHAPTER TWENTY

Tombstone
April 1881

An anonymous telegram reached me in early April, informing me my brother Jim's life was in peril over a dispute with his business partner and an employee of their establishment. While serving as Dodge city marshal, Jim entered into partnership with a man named Peacock for part ownership of The Lady Gay Saloon — not to be confused with the previously mentioned Lady Gay of Texas. It strikes me there may be a limited number of serviceable saloon names, and, for reason unknown, Lady Gay must be numbered among them. I digress. The telegram made plain Jim's life was in peril at the hands of Peacock and a man named Updegraff. The prospect evoked painful memories of Ed's killing. I'd not been able to save him. Time and distance ruled against my chances to aid Jim. Still, I had to try.

I immediately resigned my position at the Oriental with regrets to Wyatt, who perfectly understood my predicament. I caught the next stage to Benson. The arduous journey back to Dodge cannot be made hasty by urgency. Mile after mile by stage and rail I troubled over the fear I might be too late. For better or worse, I determined to save my brother's life or avenge it. The prospect it might lead to revenge did nothing to soothe my frustration as the days rolled by. Finally, the conductor announced Dodge City next. What to do?

Dodge City
April 16, 1881
As the train began its slow roll into Dodge, it occurred to me I had no idea what I might walk into disembarking at the station. I doubted anyone anticipated my return; still, word travels fast, even on the frontier. Not being an anonymous person, one never knew who might puzzle out my intended destination and purpose. To avoid any risk of advance warning as to my arrival, I made my way to the rear of the last car and stepped off the train opposite the station platform before the train reached a stop. In this fashion I could walk alongside the train

without being seen from the station. The instinct may have saved my life.

As the train rolled to a stop, I came up behind both persons of my interest there to meet the train. They remained intent upon observing passengers disembarking. I concluded they were most certainly looking for me. I held my ground, allowing arriving and departing passengers to clear the platform. I had little doubt the pair intended violence against my person. When they concluded I was not among the arriving passengers, they continued on up the station platform.

I hailed them to halt. They took one look at me in recognition and ducked into an alley next to the jail on the south side of the tracks. From there they commenced shooting. I dove behind the road-bed embankment and returned fire. In a matter of moments, sympathizers of Peacock, and the man who proved to be his brother-in-law, opened fire from the south-side sporting district. Bullets flying over my head chewed their way into businesses on north Front Street. This prompted some north-side partisans to weigh in either on my behalf or in their own defense. A full-scale gun battle then raged across the central avenue of town.

When we'd expended our allotted ammunition, the pause to reload carried the benefit of reason along with the arrival of law enforcement. The shooting fell silent. Fortunately, the gun battle fell short of the dead line designation. The only casualty was a wound to Updegraff, for which I claim no credit.

I was promptly arrested, my protest at not having started the fracas notwithstanding. Much to my relief, I found my brother to be in the pink of health. Jim visited me in jail that night, bringing in supper from a favorite restaurant to spare me the ravages of jail fare. The following morning, I paid my fine for discharging firearms in the city, whereupon my brother and I took the better of it and left town without fully appreciating we'd added a colorful chapter to Dodge City lore, a chapter that would come to be known as "the Battle of the Plaza."

Trinidad, Colorado
May 1882
After leaving Dodge I headed to Colorado, picking up the action in Trinidad. I thought about returning to Tombstone. As things turned out, I probably should have; but all that was in the future. At the time, Trinidad offered all the gaming opportunities to be found in Tombstone without the rigors of

that grueling return trip. Wyatt never held it against me. If he had, I got a chance to make it up to him soon enough.

Like most boom towns, Trinidad offered choices of places to play — the Imperial, Tivoli, and Exchange all being popular — but the high-stakes crowd hung out at the rightly named Bonanza Saloon. There I was happily at play when Wyatt Earp hit town the following spring. I'd read newspaper reports of the O.K. Corral fight and the eventual exoneration of the Earp brothers. Later reports of Virgil being shot and Morgan's assassination were sketchy, but I sympathized with the effect both must have had on Wyatt. I'd seen little reported on the events that followed. Wyatt arrived in Trinidad in company of the posse who'd accompanied him on the bloody trail later colorfully sensationalized as Wyatt's vendetta ride. Wyatt recounted the story over drinks and dinner.

When the smoke cleared after the O.K. Corral fandango, the McLaury brothers and Billy Clanton lay dead. Old man Ike Clanton got away. He and his outlaw pals plotted revenge on Wyatt and his brothers. There would be no more face to face confrontations. The first incident took place when city marshal Virgil Earp was gunned down from ambush while making his rounds. Curly Bill Brocius destroyed Virgil's left arm with a shotgun blast. Curly Bill, thinking he'd killed the elder Earp, made his escape.

A short time later, Morgan Earp was assassinated while shooting pool at a billiard parlor he favored. This time the circumstances implicated Frank Stillwell, Pete Spence, and a Mexican rustler. Wyatt saw it for a blood feud and vowed to take vengeance on all those responsible. He set out for a ranch hideout known to harbor fugitive Cowboys accompanied by Doc Holliday, youngest brother, Jim Earp, and a few competent friends. They caught up with the Mexican at the hideout and left his body for buzzard bait loaded with buckshot.

Wyatt and Doc caught up with Frank Stilwell in Tucson. When Wyatt confronted him, Stillwell knew what he'd come for. He reached for his gun. Wyatt killed him. A short time later the posse collared Indian Charlie near Tombstone. Charlie confessed to his part in Morgan's killing. Wyatt put a bullet in him. They had more trouble tracking Curly Bill Brocius but found him in a mountain hideout. Wyatt killed him, too.

By this time, Johnny Behan and authorities back in Tombstone had a stack of warrants on Wyatt, Doc, and the others. Wyatt said they'd come to Trinidad to scatter. Most did, not long after arriving. Wyatt stayed in Trinidad with me for a spell, while Doc went north looking for action at the tables in Pueblo and Denver. Doc's luck ran out in Denver when he was arrested and held for extradition on a Behan arrest warrant.

When word of Doc's arrest reached us, Wyatt took the news with grave concern. Should Doc fall into Behan's clutches, he was a dead man. Wyatt was determined to do something to help his friend. In truth there wasn't much he could do without getting himself arrested. I became the obvious choice to see what could be done for Doc.

I didn't much care for Doc Holliday. He could be arrogant, unpredictable, and of violent temperament when he'd had too much to drink, which was most of the time. I put up with the man because of my friendship with Wyatt, and the fact that, for whatever reason, my friend was close to the irascible Holliday. I'd put personal feelings aside to help Billy Thompson out of friendship for his brother Ben. It wasn't a great leap then to help Holliday as a favor to Wyatt.

Runyon listened in rapt attention. "Were you able to help him?"

I nodded.

"Did you break him out of jail?"

"Not exactly."

"Then what did you do?"

"Lady Justice is blind you know. Sometimes a fella can take that to advantage."

"I don't understand."

"I should think you would, considering the crowd you associate yourself with, present company excluded, of course."

"Of course. I still don't understand, though."

"Of course not. I caught the next stage north out of Trinidad for Denver." *Stage travel, even the memory is disagreeable.* "Hated it."

"Hated what?"

"Stage travel. Ever done much of it?"

"Cabs in the city."

"Not the same. I don't recommend it."

"Cabs?"

"No, stage travel. When it's hot, it's hot and dusty. Like to choke a man to death. When it rains things get wet and muddy. Worse when you gotta get out and walk or push."

190

"Push?"

"Third-class passengers have to if called upon, owing to a steep grade or road conditions. Pushing can get downright unpleasant."

"What about second class?"

"Only have to walk."

"What's the value of buying a ticket to ride?"

"That's first class, unless conditions become extreme. When things get that bad, the only one guaranteed a seat is the driver."

"So far I don't recommend it, either."

"I suppose not. Wait until we get to the hard part."

"What then?"

"When it's cold, you freeze your ass off. While we're down there where a man sits, I can tell you horse-hide seats are the equines' revenge on those who abused them in life. Those seats aren't built to absorb all the bounce and sway those old roads impart. If all that weren't enough, they jam six people on two benches fit for four. If you're lucky they sit you next to a pretty woman. Most of them are too smart to travel by stage. Most times they sit you next to a drummer whose linen hasn't seen a washtub in more than a month. Worst time I had, they parked me in the middle once between two of those

Jaspers. One of them tended to the portly side. He needed his share of the bench and a good part of mine, too. Bought a bottle at the first stop and put up a John Barleycorn defense the rest of the trip."

"If it's so uncomfortable, why'd you travel by stage?"

"It's fast. You go horseback, the air's fresher, but you make thirty, maybe forty, miles a day with plenty of stops to rest the horse and worry about his feed and water. Stage runs right along, changing horses every ten miles or so. Somebody else worries about care and feed. Most travel through the night, so you make miles even while you're sleeping.

"The run up to Pueblo gave me time to think how the hell I might get Doc out of his jam. Somewhere in the small hours of the first night out, she hiked up her scarf and winked at me."

"A woman winked at you?"

"Not just any woman, Lady Justice. I stopped off in Pueblo for a day."

CHAPTER TWENTY-ONE

I was acquainted with the city marshal in Pueblo and thought he might extend me a favor. Turned out I didn't need it. I explained the circumstances of Doc's incarceration and the risks of his extradition to Arizona. I offered to file a complaint against Doc the marshal might use to obtain custody of the prisoner. Turned out I didn't need to file a complaint; the marshal already had a warrant for Doc on another charge. He was pleased to learn of his whereabouts and forthwith wired the sheriff in Denver requesting custody. Sheriff Spangler in Denver refused.

I boarded the next stage to Denver, curious as to why Sheriff Spangler refused to honor a Colorado jurisdiction and still no closer to a remedy than when I'd arrived in Pueblo.

Denver

As it turned out I wasn't the only one interested in gaining custody of Doc. We knew back in Cochise County, Johnny Behan petitioned the Arizona territorial governor for extradition authority to obtain custody of Holliday. Bob Paul, now Pima County sheriff, also petitioned the governor for similar authority. The governor favored Paul's appeal, and the sheriff headed for Denver to claim his prisoner.

I arrived in Denver, checked into a hotel, and made straight for the jail. A deputy admitted me to the cell block. Due to the ravages of illness and the effects of heavy drinking, Doc never looked healthful. The gray pallor of confinement did little to improve the appearance of a cadaver not yet properly embalmed. He rolled off a stained mattress on his bunk and mustered the barest hint of a smile.

"Bat," he said. "Good of you to come. Friendly faces have come in short supply here as you can plainly see."

"Wyatt asked me to see if there is anything I might do to help."

"Ah, Wyatt — a favored friend. He would."

"He'd have come himself, though that would have done little more than have him join you."

194

"I understand. He sent a good man. I do appreciate it."

For once in our usually reserved acquaintance, Holliday set aside his aloof demeanor and seemed genuinely pleased to see me. I took it for an understanding of the precarious nature of his situation.

"I hope I can help. I struck out on my first attempt."

"How so?"

"Tried to get you transferred to Pueblo on a lesser charge. The sheriff seems determined to hold you."

"Spangler's no friend of mine. He's waitin' to see me extradited to Arizona."

"Any word on that score?"

"Bob Paul is in town with an extradition order."

"What's Bob got to do with this?"

"He's Pima County sheriff now. Bob's all right, but if they get me back to Cowboy country, I wouldn't take a dime bet on my own chan—"

A coughing fit finished the thought.

"Will Spangler honor Bob's order?"

"Governor Pitkin has to officially approve it. Likely he will, as Arizona favored Bob's request over Behan's. If the governor orders it, Spangler has no choice."

"What's the delay?"

"Governor is out of town."

"That's my next move then."

"What move?"

"Get to the governor before Bob does."

With that I took my leave. I knew I couldn't just walk into the governor's office and start calling for favors. I needed an angle. A man of my acquaintance named Cowen covered the capital for the *Denver Tribune.* I figured he'd know the score.

I found him at the newspaper office late that afternoon, and sure enough he knew the situation. The governor was expected to return that evening and had yet to resume his official duties. I told Cowen I needed to see him pronto on a matter of life and death. He obliged.

Just past the supper hour I found myself sitting in the office of a bleary-eyed territorial governor. I described the situation in Tombstone and the peril it posed to Doc's life. I appealed to his sense of justice in a man maintaining his innocence until proven guilty by a jury of his peers. Justice did not abide assassination or lynching at the hands of partisans with erstwhile motivation. I explained the sheriff in Pueblo had a legitimate warrant for Doc and that his request to take custody had been denied by Sheriff Spangler, who appeared to favor Arizona's

lethal claim, the last assertion being speculation on my part. The governor allowed as
how he would consider it.

Likely Bob Paul reached the governor's
office the next day with his extradition
order. The governor subsequently ordered
Doc turned over to face the charges awaiting him in Pueblo. He cited a flaw in the
form of the Arizona order and the jurisdic-
tional superiority of Colorado's claim, possession in this case being nine-tenths of the
law.

I stayed around Denver, visiting Doc and
playing some cards, until the sheriff arrived
from Pueblo. Bob Paul returned to Tombstone, somewhat relieved, I think, to be
discharged of a duty he regarded as the best
of a bad lot. I accompanied Doc and the
sheriff to Pueblo, where Doc promptly
posted bond against his charge and was
released. He successfully avoided prosecution throughout the remainder of his days.

Metropole Hotel
Forty-Second and Broadway
Runyon stubbed out his cigarette and
drained the dregs of his coffee. He glanced
at his watch.

"Got a tip to cover."

"Some bank about to be robbed?"

197

"An interesting story. You of all people should understand."

"I cover sporting events."

"So do I, sometimes. You made plenty of interesting stories back in the day. It's how you came by your notoriety. Folks like me reported on you and your friends for the interesting things you did. That's how you got that colorful reputation of yours."

"I suppose. Those days are bygone now, and my friends are mostly gone, too."

"They are, except for you and Wyatt, and you're both domesticated. Your interesting stories are back in the day."

"Today, not as interesting as your hot tip."

"Time and a place for everything."

He winked and slid out of the booth. "See you for lunch."

"O-kay."

I watched him depart through the sea of patrons at the bar. Waved the waiter for another Manhattan. I savored the warmth of a swallow. All this reminiscing had me given to nostalgia. I'd gone back to Trinidad after settling Doc in Pueblo. Trinidad in '82 held other memories. *Emma.*

Emma Walters, blonde hair, blue eyes, sang like lark. Understood me like no other woman before or since. Still does. She had me off my feet before I knew what hit me and let me think it happened the other way around. Still does that, too. Now I know when I've been had. I can't be fooled as easy as I once could; I just don't mind anymore. We eased into husband and wife before we ever bothered to put a ceremonial ribbon on it. Most women wouldn't hold with that. We were so much alike it was enough for her. Made things real comfortable. We had plenty of time to come to some matrimonial arrangement.

Remarkable woman, Emma. Ready for anything, strait-laced decorum notwithstanding. She didn't mind my gambling. We shared a sense of adventure I'd never found in a woman before. Still do, though our adventures now come in tamer varieties. I think that's what made us soul mates. They say everyone has one. In my case, I'd have bet against it. I'd have lost that bet, too. I've been known to lose some good bets, as we'll see, should Runyon persist in meandering down the dusty corridors of my memories. Glad I lost that bet. I might have lost, but I walked away with the winner's share of the prize.

I drained my glass. Checked my watch. Emma waitin' supper. I tossed a double eagle on the table, enough to cover Runyon's tab and tip. I slid out of the booth and headed for the chill autumn evening.

CHAPTER TWENTY-TWO

Morning Telegraph

Mornings at the *Telegraph* tended to be quiet. Evening deadlines for a morning publication could be chaotic, but, once the morning edition went to bed, things quieted down until the chaos started all over again. Owing to my years making a living at the gaming tables, I'm not much of a morning person. Late mornings I could usually be found at my desk when I had a column coming due. A man could think without undue interruption. I'd had my hand to the grindstone for a couple of hours as lunchtime approached. Runyon dropped in unexpectedly and caught me wrapping up one of my views on a timely topic whose time has surely passed.

"The master at work," he announced himself.

I swiveled my chair. "Slumming? No, wait . . . this is uptown. Slumming comes after dark."

"Just happened to be in the neighborhood. My stomach thought we might rescue you from your labors."

"Your stomach thinks. I should never have guessed."

"Lunch?"

"A man must sustain himself."

"Can I ask about the tintype?"

I didn't need to ask which one. "You already have. What do you want to know?"

"Who are those men with you, and what occasioned the taking of such a picture?"

"I'd left Trinidad by that time. Moved on to Pueblo and wouldn't have given a damn what the corrupt bloodsuckers in Dodge were up to, if it hadn't been for Short."

"Luke Short?"

"The very same. Luke left Tombstone not long after I did. He went back to Dodge and took over a gambling concession at the Long Branch. He bought out Chalk Beeson's share in the place in early '83. The Long Branch always was a popular saloon with the Texas trail herd crews. Luke being a Texan only added to the popularity. Probably added too much popularity, as Short would tell it. He and his partner, Bill Harris, started taking too large a share of business to suit Mayor A. B. Webster, who owned the next-door Alamo Saloon, and George Hoover, who owned the liquor store on the other side. Webster ran the city council along with city attorney Mike Sutton, the city marshal, and the sheriff."

"Sounds like a topic best finished at Lundy's."

"Lundy's. Am I never to make you a man of discriminating taste?"

"Am I never to make you a true denizen of Broadway and a man of the Great White Way?"

"I'm a Broadway guy. Merely one with good taste. Speaking of taste, nice tie."

"I'm rather fond of it."

"Let's go to lunch. Perhaps you may do yourself a favor and spill soup on it."

"You can't find this tie in the garment district."

"Of course not. The shop that sold it was condemned for a public nuisance."

"And you lecture me on taste."

"I do or, more particularly, an absence of it."

Dodge City
April 1883
Webster decided not to run for reelection as mayor in the spring of '83. His hand-picked successor, a man named Deger, who would

serve as his stooge, easily won election. Less than a month after the election, the city council enacted ordinances designed to take the wind out of Short's sails. The ordinances prohibited prostitution and vagrancy. Luke wasn't troubled by the notion at first. Hell, gambling was technically illegal in Dodge. Those ordinances were enforced with fines when the city needed an increase in tax receipts. They were ignored when the city coffers were in balance. Luke figured the new laws for little more than a new tax by a different name. When his working girls were arrested, he figured to pay the fines and get back to business as usual. Things didn't quite work out that way. Come to find out, Luke's girls were the only ones being arrested. It turned out his business was the only business subject to enforcement of the new ordinances. Webster and Hoover weren't troubled by any of it. At first, neither were any of the other gaming concessions or cribs in town. Luke, it seemed, had ordinance enforcement all to himself.

At that point, he strapped on his guns and marched off to the jail determined to get his girls back. A city policeman loitering outside the jail saw an armed gunslinger coming his way with fire in his eye. He panicked and in a fool's moment pulled his gun, fired once, and decided better to make a run for it. Luke cut loose one shot, and the officer tripped on the boardwalk and fell, leading Short to believe he'd shot the man. Knowing the politics of law enforcement in Dodge where he was concerned, he retreated to the Long Branch and forted up with a shotgun as a deterrent to any would-be arresting officers.

None of the city's finest had any interest in flushing a heavily armed Luke Short out of his fort. The city marshal finally convinced Luke to give it up, explaining he hadn't killed the cowardly cop, he'd only scared him half to death, and that could be settled for a misdemeanor fine. Luke took the offer at face value and surrendered his guns. Once he stepped into the street unarmed, he was arrested and marched off to jail charged with assault with intent to kill. That charge was a long sight worse than a misdemeanor.

With Short subdued, Webster proceeded to have his pet mayor and police force round up others whose businesses infringed on his own. When the town was cleaned out to Webster's satisfaction, the prisoners were escorted to the depot under armed guard and given the opportunity to leave peaceably or stand trial on a variety of trumped-up charges. Short faced the worst of it and once again accepted the offer. Others followed his lead exactly as Webster intended. All were loaded on a train to Kansas City.

I was in Denver at the time, where I received an urgent wire from Luke. He requested I meet him in Kansas City as a matter of utmost urgency. Not being more notably engaged at the time, I entrained for Kansas City at the next opportunity. There I found Luke with our old friend Charlie Bassett at one of Kansas City's more posh gambling emporia. The story he told set to boil old blood feuds we'd had over the years with the sanctimonious Dodge City reformers represented by Webster and his lot of cronies. The question glared at us: *what could be done to absolve such a flagrant miscarriage of justice?*

We'd all buffaloed tougher crowds than the Webster cabal, and so it was decided a show of force was needed to back them down. Firstly, we needed to deny the cowards any chance of relief. Recalling the value of my visit to the governor's office on Doc Holliday's behalf, I suggested Luke visit the governor.

May 10

Short presented his petition of grievance to Governor George Glick, prompting the governor to commence an enquiry into the situation in Dodge. The governor received assurances from the sheriff and mayor's offices that there was no disturbance in Dodge. The town hadn't enjoyed such peaceful times in years, owing to the recent departure from the community of all manner of disreputable elements. In turn the governor assured Short, with a wink, that, since matters were so well in hand in Dodge, he saw no need to intervene in whatever proceedings might ensue.

While Luke maneuvered his way through the governor's office, Charlie and I set about assembling a proper show of force. We, along with Luke, constituted a good start. To our number we added a call to Wyatt, Doc Holliday, and a few other notables of our acquaintance. We then leaked word these gentlemen were expected in Dodge in support of their friend, Luke Short. At the news, Webster's stouthearted accomplices rapidly became watery about the spine and knees.

We assembled our friends to plan our next move. It was decided that Wyatt and Doc should be the first to return to Dodge. Wyatt continued to enjoy a positive, though no less formidable, reputation with the community. From that we would see how matters might unfold and proceed accordingly from there.

Wyatt and Doc decamped for Dodge, along with Charlie, Bill Harris, and one or two others. They made their appearance and presence known along Front Street, waiting to see what Webster and his puppets might do. Faced with raw firepower certain to grow in number and menace, Mayor Deger and the city marshal petitioned Governor Glick for assistance. Glick responded he'd been given every assurance matters were fully in hand and therefore deferred to local authorities. Realization dawned on Webster and his accomplices they were in this on their own. Luke Short had no shortage of formidable friends assembling to back his play. Faced with the prospect of a showdown, Webster sent for Wyatt to discuss terms.

Luke and I received Wyatt's wire in Kansas City, informing us the mood of the city fathers had mellowed. We entrained the next day. Arriving in Dodge, we were greeted by Webster and his entourage in the spirit of bygones being bygones. Luke called a meeting with the mayor, sheriff, and city attorney to settle the fine points of a new understanding. Wyatt and I accompanied him to assure no misunderstanding later arose, whereupon Luke prevailed on the mayor to accept his terms. Policemen responsible for selective enforcement of city ordinances were to be removed from the force. He demanded and received repeal of the offending ordinances. Finally, all charges pending against Luke over the dispute were dropped, with all fines levied returned. With that, what became known as the Dodge City War ended over drinks without so much as a shot fired.

Shanley's Grill
Forty-Third and Broadway
Runyon smiled over the rim of his coffee cup.

"And the tintype?"

"We allowed as how, since we had so many of the old gang reunited, it seemed only fitting we should memorialize the occasion in a portrait."

"The Dodge City Peace Commission."

"Some call it that."

"You know it might prove valuable one day. Such historic memorabilia often do."

"When the rest of us are dead. I for one am not eager just yet to seek investment returns in photography."

"Still, it makes for a good story."

"And a decent lunch to you for a change. You can thank me now for insisting on the grill." I passed him the check. Long overdue.

CHAPTER TWENTY-THREE

Polo Grounds

Baseball should finish by August. It is a summer pastime. I'm no fan of football, never have been; but baseball in autumn? It's acceptable enough in the summer when cold beer serves a purpose. The grass grows faster than the game. Come autumn even that diversion falls out. You can't bet on it without raising the specter of scandal, the "fall classic" having been so recently tainted by those scoundrels from Chicago. In summer you had your choice of the Giants or the upstart Yankees. When it came to the championship series, you got the winner, in this case the Yankees led by a slugger and Broadway rounder they call Babe. Really, Babe? Conjures up visions of a show girl. Give me a pugilist. Why, I ask myself, am I here? And in the shadow of Harlem no less to watch a team charged with evading selective service.

Runyon insisted, I argued. He stooped so low as to accuse us of being sports writers.

I understand the accusation. The sport I write about is boxing. When it comes to baseball there is clearly not enough evidence to gain a conviction.

You're the one who agreed to come.

So I did. I hunkered down in my coat against the chill. Here I sit arguing with myself and unable, it seems, to win my own argument. I wondered at that. Not the arguing so much; I'm quite comfortable with these internal debates. After all, who better to engage me in spirited controversy than, well, me. No, the troubling part isn't the debate; it's the notion of losing to myself. I don't care for losing. No one knows that better than I. *Could it be your age is showing, old boy?* Fiddlesticks.

With the score knotted at one, Runyon rescued me from the boredom of my self-induced dilemma.

"Peanut?"

I eyed the bag. Shells got all over everything. Barroom floors and ballparks. Salty, though. Sufficient to justify a beer. I took a few and cracked the first.

"So how do you explain it?"

"Explain what?"

"Turning from gambler to sportswriter?"

212

"Much as it pains me to say it, I probably owe my present livelihood to a vulgarian excuse for a newspaper man known as Otto Floto and his column at *The Denver Post.* His particular brand of double dealing self-promotion necessitated the sort of response that put a pen in my hand."

"Vulgarian was he? High regard coming from you."

"The man would steal the pennies off a dead man's eyes."

"That is vulgar. Who is he?"

"A man who cheated me out of a share in promoting the fight game in Denver."

"If you owe your journalistic career to a fellow journalist, why hold him in such contempt?"

"Journalist? Charlatan is more like it. He cheated me. He cheated the paying public who attended the square dances he called boxing exhibitions, and he used his position at *The Denver Post* to do it. What's to admire in vermin like that?"

"Well, if you dislike him so, how do you credit him with your journalistic endeavors?"

"Self-defense. I couldn't shoot the bloated porker. All I could do to defend the competitions I brought against his was to seat myself as a sportswriter on a small weekly and beat him at his own unscrupulous game. After that, the blood feud between us got bad."

"You mean he attacked you personally?"

"We came to fisticuffs once."

"How did that turn out?"

"Otto Bloato ran like he'd blundered into a pen with an angry bull."

"I see. So, it was a business dispute that brought you to a career in sports writing?"

"Not exactly. Gambling and a pack of sanctimonious reformers did that."

"Gambling and reformers. Now I am confused."

"Nothing confusing about it. When reformers preached, politicked, and editorialized the evils of every sporting pursuit from gaming to demon rum, the only recourse we had was letters to the editors of any daily that dared to print my views. It taught me I could acquit myself about as well with a pen as I could with a gun. Cut Bloato a new one more than a few times, I did." I had to smile at that — Otto Floto hoisted on his own petard as it were. Got him with an ink pot and pen. Minor consolation for the ruination of prize fighting in Denver.

"And gambling?"

"Do you stay up nights dreaming up questions to pester me with? You need a woman or some other vice to occupy your mind. Gambling led me to sports. You can gamble on prize fights, horse races, foot races, you name it. Why, in those days, you could even bet on baseball, or football if you had the stomach for it. I cut my teeth on cards. Made my living at faro, until the prohibitionists got the high and mighty of it.

"Boxing had a natural appeal to me. It is a manly art. People had a hunger to follow it in print and read of the results. Once I figured out you could make book on the sport, it wasn't long before I saw opportunity to handicap the fighters and their matches. Turns out people will pay to read expert opinion. Pugilistic expertise paid two ways. It paid in words, and it paid in wagers, the words being a less risky bargain."

"So, prohibitionists and a bad business deal made a sports writer out of a gambler."

"That's about the size of it."

"Do you suppose he'd be pleased to know that?"

"I'd be pleased if he still had trouble sitting where I cut him the last time."

The crack of a bat caught him up in his note pad as the ball arced gracefully over the fence in right field. I watched the stocky ball player some called the Sultan of Swat waddle around the bases. A moment to savor. I shelled another peanut and thought about a beer.

Morning Telegraph
November 11, 1919

I dated the story in time to make my editor's deadline as the office faded to golden sepia edged in soft shadow. You always date a story. It was the eleventh; a March 11th was an eleventh I remembered. Dates mark the passage of time. Funny how that is with old men. My thoughts drifted. Ben Thompson was a friend. He'd likely saved my life that January night at the Lady Gay down in Sweetwater in '76. King . . . Corporal Melvin King — that was his name. I remembered drawing and firing. Mollie caught King's bullet. So did I. I'd 'a likely caught more than that if it hadn't been for Ben getting the drop on King's pals. Ben backed my play at the Royal Gorge dust-up, too. He didn't need to ask twice for my help with the scrape that no-account brother of his got into back in '80. Damn shame the way they killed him that March 11th in '84.

Following the Royal Gorge war, Ben opened a gambling parlor in the Iron Front Saloon in Austin, Texas. The following year he was elected city marshal. About that time, while on a business trip to San Antonio, Ben became involved in a dispute over gambling losses with a man named Foster, part owner in a gambling hall and theater establishment known as the Vaudeville Theater. Foster and his partner, Jack Harris, made it clear to anyone who would listen Thompson was no longer welcome in their place of business.

Ben wasn't one to back down. On his next trip to San Antonio — when was that? Summer of '82 seems about right — Ben returned to the Vaudeville. He ordered a drink and told the bartender to let Foster and Harris know he was in the bar. Finished with his drink, he stepped outside to converse with a passerby. Harris appeared in the bar armed with a shotgun. He observed Thompson and waited. Ben spotted Harris and demanded to know what he intended to do with the shotgun. Pleasantries were exchanged and shots fired. Harris fell mortally wounded.

Allegations of murder against Thompson were vociferously tried in newspapers, San Antonio, representing the prosecution and Austin the defense. A court finally ruled in January 1883. Ben was acquitted, to the delight of his supporters and the wrath of his detractors. Bad blood simmered for more than a year.

On March 11, 1884, while again in San Antonio on business, Ben ran into long-time friend and notable gun hand King Fisher. The two old friends spent a pleasant evening together, attending a play. Later, likely buoyed by the evening's libations, they stopped in at the Vaudeville Theater. Ben asked to see Joe Foster, perhaps in hope of putting hostilities to rest after the passage of so much time. Under the circumstances, an invitation to meet two of the West's most accomplished gunmen must certainly have provoked some skepticism, even more so if the intent was to avenge the death of Jack Harris.

Thompson and Fisher were invited to accompany Foster's new partner to meet in Foster's theater box. They did so and were greeted with an uneasy atmosphere. When Foster made no move to amenity, Fisher sensed something amiss. He and Ben leaped to their feet to exit the box too late. Instead they met a volley of assassins' bullets fired from another box. Ben went down. Someone in the box finished him with a pistol shot to the head.

As one might imagine, accounts of what happened that night are one-sided. Foster was wounded in the fight, lost a leg, and died on the operating table. The only other certainty is that Ben Thompson, and King Fisher for having been with Ben, were gunned down from ambush by faceless assassins who would never be held to account.

I filed my story and headed for the Metropole in need of a drink. The glow in the office cast an illusion of warmth unceremoniously dismissed by a brisk north wind cutting Broadway. I ducked inside and made it to my usual booth before the five o'clock crowd overtook preferred seating. I ordered a whiskey Manhattan to take off the chill.

I noticed her come in across the smoky bar on the arm of one of Runyon's hoodlum chums. The suit, cigar, and attractive doll conspired with the toney Metropole to invest the pair with an aura of respectability. Golden curls, shapely figure set my mind adrift.

CHAPTER TWENTY-FOUR

California Hall
Denver
September 1886

Nellie McMahon. Fresh-as-a-flower skin, golden curls, and laughing blue eyes with a husky voice that could breathe out a ballad fit to make . . . make a man out of you. I was enraptured. She invited me to her private box for the second act. It mattered not her husband, comedian Lou Spencer, was the second act. I climbed the stairs to the curtained box intoxicated by the scent of her and a come-hither, coquettish invitation fit to put a shine in a man's eyes.

The second act opened with a few fluttered lashes. She made no pretense at an exchange of sweet nothings. We went to kissing like red bloods in heat, which, as it turned out, we were. Emma slipped my mind. I have a fair idea of what was on Nellie's mind when she climbed on my lap before the second act curtain call. The jokes failed to intrude on our heated acquaintance. I should have paid attention to the applause. I neglected that in favor of more pressing affairs, at least until the draperies parted abruptly to Lou Spencer's extreme displeasure.

He had some rather unflattering things to say to his wife. I don't suppose I begrudged him that, though he clearly begrudged me my part in the unseemly affair. One thing led to another as such things often do. Fisticuffs overtook civility, unfortunately for Spencer, as he was no match for me in my prime. Someone summoned the bouncer, followed soon thereafter by a city policeman. Neither arrived in time to save Spencer from my defense but soon enough to see to my incarceration for disorderly conduct. Fined and embarrassed I returned to my Emma, who laughed off my embarrassment without knowing the lurid details. That didn't last long.

Owing to my reputation, coupled with Nellie and Spencer's fame, the police blotter caught the attention of the local dailies. Emma was furious, a condition that only worsened two days later when Nellie filed for divorce. Her perfumed note — I have never forgotten the scent — arrived to find me firmly frozen in Emma's accusatory dog house. Whereupon, I admit to doing the only thing reasonable to a red blood in heat. In a fit of cupidity, I ran off to Kansas City with Nellie, where we picked up at the third act and carried on to ardent excess for a few more days. Once we'd slaked our appetites, things sobered up. Heat wasn't love. We'd had a fine fling, but flings run their course. Faced with the fact of exhausted fascination, we went our separate ways.

Contrite, I returned to Denver and Emma's scorn intent on collecting my things. As expected, I got a chilly reception. I told her I'd foolishly been caught up in the moment. It hadn't amounted to more than . . . well, the basest of . . . well, you know, base. She shed a tear or two. Quite unlike her. Her tears moved me more to shame and sorrow than the chill of her anger. I set myself to packing my belongings. That didn't last long. She stomped a foot and said she didn't want me to go. I said I didn't want to leave and again professed my sincerest sorrow. And then, by graces I neither deserve nor understand, she forgave me. We made our amends more lovingly than the heat in the moments that lead me astray. I have never after that wavered from the straight and narrow of our union.

I've never regretted the decision we came to that day, though I confess I needed a second Manhattan to recover from the memory of that fiery fling in Kansas City before Runyon arrived out of breath.

"Sorry. I'm running late."

"FBI interview?"

"Please. Why would the feds have the least interest in your humble servant?"

"Just a guess based on your made man over there." I lifted my chin to the guy and his doll.

"Joey? Small potatoes for the feds."

"Well, that clears things up."

"If you must know, I was working on a story and lost track of time."

"Gainful employment is to be admired."

"Speaking of gainful, for all your gambling days and all the parlors you played, is there one that stands out in your recollection?"

I didn't have to think long on that one.

"Luke Short's White Elephant in Fort Worth. Most elegant gambling hall in all of the West. Comes with a story to boot."

Runyon smiled as the waiter appeared with a steaming cup of coffee. He tapped out a cigarette and lit up, ready for more.

Luke cashed out his Dodge City game shortly after the Dodge City War ended. He declared his intent to return to Texas and find a new gaming parlor. He packed his bags and headed back to Texas, with me tagging along to assist him in selecting a gaming concession. We found a spectacular gambling palace in Fort Worth suited to his taste. The owner sold him the gaming concession, certain his reputation would attract the high-rollers of the day. It did. Wyatt and I may have had a hand in that, as we both found play at the White Elephant inviting when visiting Fort Worth.

Luke soon discovered Dodge City hadn't cornered the market on corrupt politicians and law dogs. Fort Worth had its own band of fixers, riggers, and shenanigan purveyors. Chief among them was former sheriff Timothy Isiah Courtright, known to some as "Longhair Jim" for reasons unknown. After vacating slopping at the public trough, Courtright supported himself by running a protection racket. He charged local businesses for his "security services," which amounted to an agreement he would not do them any damage so long as they paid for it. Luke provided his own protection. He wasn't intimidated by Courtright's threats and had no interest in paying the thug extortion money. He thus put Courtright in an awkward position. If Luke didn't pay, others might decide they could defy his racket as well.

Matters came to a head one night in February 1887. I happened to be in the White Elephant that night upstairs with Luke minding his games. He'd filled me in on his impending troubles with the former sheriff, though neither of us expected anything to come of it so soon. Word came up from the saloon, Courtright was out front demanding to see Luke. We exchanged glances. I still remember the look in Short's eye; I'd seen it before. Good sense didn't mess with that look. I followed him downstairs.

Courtright had been drinking his courage. He eyed me and suggested he and Luke take a walk. Luke gave me a nod and started down the block toward a shooting gallery south of the White Elephant. Courtright made it clear that rejecting his offer of protection was not an option. He informed Luke that if he were to accuse Luke of threatened violence, no one would question the fact he'd killed him. Luke allowed as how Courtright's claim of having killed him seemed somewhat premature, whereupon Courtright drew. In what I account a measure of human kindness over poor shooting, Luke shot the racketeer's thumb off. Courtright next added blind rage to stupidity by flipping his gun to his left hand, whereupon Luke shot him five times, killing him before he hit the pavement.

One might suppose that put an end to bad business, but such was not to be the case. Luke was arrested and hustled off to jail until a court might decide if charges were warranted. I accompanied him, though not to be locked up. For all his disreputable deeds, Courtright had more than a few friends in town. I became concerned Luke's case might never come before a court of law. A lynch mob seemed more likely. The sheriff saw it the same way, though he had little appetite for facing off against his angered constituents in anything other than the next election. I suggested he lock Luke up armed and allow me to spend the night with him. The sheriff was quick to grasp a way out of his dilemma, meeting me halfway. He didn't lock Luke up armed, but he did allow me to spend the night armed. He then spread the word to those disgruntled by Courtright's death that any attempt to exact impromptu hemp justice would be confronted by two of the West's most accomplished shootists. No mob materialized that night. By morning, cooler heads prevailed.

Luke was arraigned before a grand jury. As expected, the jury ruled self-defense.

Metropole Hotel
Forty-Second and Broadway
Runyon scratched a note on his ever-present pad.

"There's that reputation again."

"It did come in handy from time to time."

He glanced at his watch. "Got to run. I'll come by for lunch Friday." He got up to go.

I weighed a cold walk against the prospect of another Manhattan and signaled the bartender.

Luke set a small, though valuable, precedent. So many friends who lived by the gun, died by the gun. Luke Short was one of the best in any situation that went to gun play. The Courtright affair ended his gunfighting days. He continued his business as a professional gambler, investing in the ownership of various gaming establishments. In prosperity, he eventually married and settled down to a life of domestic bliss.

Suffering from consumption in '93, he traveled with his wife to Geuda Springs,

Kansas. There he sought curative relief from the therapeutic hot springs located there. He died in his sleep September eighth. They buried him in Fort Worth in the very cemetery where he planted Longhair Jim Courtright. Luke died in bed of natural causes. That left Wyatt and me. These days, times being what they are, it looks like the two of us might make it to our natural causes, too.

CHAPTER TWENTY-FIVE

Morning Telegraph

For some reason, late morning light turned a dirty yellow in the newsroom. Might have been the soot on the windows. I'd poured myself a cup of the dishwater that passed for coffee and regretted it the moment the steam cooled off. Lead story in the morning edition prattled on prospects for enacting a prohibition on the production, sale, and consumption of strong drink. *Reformers.* There was something fundamentally wrong with people who couldn't abide another person's enjoyment. We got a taste of it back in Dodge, a hefty helping in Denver, and now it appeared as though the worst of them were about to infect the entire country. This time the empty shoe-shines conspired with the fire and brimstone clergy crowd and cretin politicians firmly in the pockets of the sanctimonious self-righteous in a union to threaten another man's right to enjoy a drink. I shook my head, thinking back to Denver and the days a little John Barleycorn lubricated the games at my tables. *The Palace Variety Theater.*

Short's White Elephant may have been elegant, but the Palace wasn't far behind. I suppose Luke's success in Fort Worth influenced my decision to buy the place. I kind of fell in love the moment I stepped into it. Let's see . . . that must have been '88. The bar room glittered like a diamond mine. All the dark wood and glass pricked by stars from a massive crystal chandelier. Twenty-five tables covered in green felt provided play for as many as two hundred high-rollers. You could have entertained royalty in the theater. Done in red velvet, it sat seven hundred, with luxury boxes for those who paid for privacy. I didn't mind collecting rent on them. Personally, I'd sworn off that particular temptation for the sake of my union with Emma. We catered food and beverage to the boxes during the shows. Booked some of the best vaudeville acts of the day, too. First class entertainment out on the frontier; nothing but the best at Bat Masterson's Palace. Might still be there, too, if it hadn't been for them sons-a . . . Never use profanity myself. No penman worthy the claim would where pedantic eloquence might suffice. Like taking a knife to a gunfight. I digress. If it hadn't been for those who call themselves *reformers.* Self-righteous moralists, bible thumpers, and political humbugs in perpetual pursuit of reelection is more like it. Purveyors of tedious ill-humor every last one of them. Keen to inflict their version of propriety on the rest of us, where personal liberty and jocularity ought prevail. Not a convivial shard of humanity amongst the lot of them. The worst are given journalistic license to promote this brand of rubbish, followed closely by that mindless class of bureaucrats who have nothing better to do than enact into law platitudes of steaming bovine pie chips. At least those who rage from the pulpit do so on the strength of principled conviction. I only quarrel with the need to impose their will on the lives of those less inclined to such stringent adherence to strictures of their belief. By '91 they'd all but run us out of business.

All this disagreeable reflection soured my disposition. It seems it showed when Runyon stopped by for lunch.

"Look at you, sitting there like you'd just swallowed a spoonful of mole-asses. What's the matter?"

I handed him the paper and pointed to

the Prohibition story. "Reformist foolery," I said.

"Ah. Being acquainted with the wages of demon rum, I understand the moral intent."

"You are perfectly free to indulge your understanding of it. It isn't necessary for such understanding to deny the rest of us our indulgence."

"It's for your own good, the reformer would say."

"And who is a better judge of my good than me? Come on. Shanley's for lunch. I need a drink before it is prohibited to me."

Outside winter had fallen sharply on a chill breeze. We marched up Broadway to Forty-third. We'd beaten the rush of the lunch crowd and were shown to a pleasant table looking out on the city blustering by on a gusty wind. I ordered a Manhattan, as much out of spite for the proposed nonsense as a remedy to my chill. Runyon warmed his hands on his coffee cup studying the menu. I ordered the special, shepherd's pie, and took a swallow of my rebellious beverage.

"It will likely be good for business," Runyon said with a wry smile.

"Good for business?"

"Prohibition, I mean."

"How could denying a man his libation

be good for business?"

"You don't really expect people to stop drinking, do you?"

"If you make booze illegal . . ." I paused and got the picture. "You've been talking to some of your . . . shall we say, less reputable friends."

He smiled. "Some think booze will be big business. Some actually side with the reformers you so despise for reasons others might regard as perverse. They've even backed the political powers that be to encourage the opening of a . . . shall we say, new market."

My mood mellowed and not yet from the Manhattan. "And there you have it. Proof positive politicians are little more than hoodlums themselves. Still, we shall invent new outlets, won't we?"

"Likely at a somewhat higher price, given the forbidden nature of the fruit, but fruit nonetheless. I suspect you've found your way around reform before."

I nodded. "It's true, when gaming dried up in the West, the sports merely moved along to new amusements."

"Tell me about it."

"By '91, they'd all but run us out of the gaming business. We got a brief reprieve in the form of a silver strike in Creede, Colorado. Boom towns boom. Sooner or later most bust. Be it cattle, gold, or silver, the rails move on, the veins peter out, the reformers move in, and the fortune seekers move on. We were running out of boom towns in the early '90's. When Creede went bust, it left us to wonder what might be next.

"Gaming is an appetite for risk, chance, and wager. If it wasn't to be found by play at a deck of cards, or the turn of a wheel or the roll of a die, some new amusement must be found. It took no time at all for gentlemen of the sporting fraternity to find new fun, this time in the confines of a pugilist boxing ring."

"And that's what got you started on your new career?"

"Actually, my interest in boxing started back in '82 on a trip to New Orleans. Paddy Ryan, a fighter who claimed to be American heavyweight champion, scheduled a title fight with an up and coming kid from Boston by the name of Sullivan."

"The great John L. Sullivan was a kid?"

"You say 'great.' "

"You don't?"

"Hardly. Creature of his own press clippings."

"You mean he didn't deserve his reputation?"

"Not, in our humble opinion, based on his record."

"Well, I suppose you know something about inflated reputation."

"More importantly, I know the manly art of boxing, a skill that largely eluded said Sullivan."

"I'll concede that argument for the moment. He still won the fight. You say Ryan claimed to be the heavyweight champ; was he or wasn't he?"

"He was until somebody beat him. Ryan was a heavy favorite. I'm a gambler. I admit I liked the look of the Sullivan kid before we knew more about his boxing proficiency. He was built like a brawler with hands that packed both thunder and lightning. There was plenty of action to be had on that side of the card. It took him nine rounds, but the kid put Ryan away. Knocked him out cold. People were stunned. Sullivan was heavyweight champion of America. Boxing as we know it today was born out of that bout."

Recollection brought a smile with it. And I made a killing.

"My reputation with a gun got me into the game big time in '89. Pony Moore hired me to bodyguard Jake Kilrain in the run-up to a heavyweight title fight with Sullivan."

"Why'd he need a bodyguard?"

"To keep things square. You of all people should understand that."

Arriving in New Orleans you might say we hit town, but it would be more accurate to say the town hit us with a stifling wall of stinking, sea-soaked air. It was then we learned reformers, terrified at the prospect of a prize fight defiling their midst, prevailed on the city politicrats to ban pugilistic contests. The fight had to be moved across the state line to Mississippi, where it could take place the following day. Trains were chartered to convey the fighters, their entourages, sport enthusiasts, and the press to the small town of Ritchburg, some four hours by rail from New Orleans and, for purposes of the fight, beyond the reach of the reformers and their authorities.

Neither heat nor air were mitigated by the Mississippi state line. The fighters stepped into the ring under a blazing sun. Kilrain was a thoroughbred fighter in peak condition. He needed to be. Sullivan was considered the best bare-knuckle brawler ever to tread the canvas. The fighters logged seventy-five rounds over better than two and a quarter hours.

Seventy-five rounds seems unheard of by today's fight game, but bare-knuckle bouts were fought under London prize ring rules. A round ended when either opponent went down. This resulted in a thirty-second respite before the fight resumed with a new round. Fighters were entitled to go down, following contact by their opponent. "Contact" is not to be confused with a telling blow; a push, a slap, or a body bump sufficed. One other convention of the bare-knuckle bout bears mention. It was customary for each competitor, on entering the ring, to place a wager on himself, the stake to be held by the referee. Kilrain and Sullivan each wagered a thousand dollars on themselves to win. Both conventions would come into play in this fight.

Kilrain was a skilled pugilist. He jabbed with his left and crossed with his right, textbook strategy that delivered negligible effect to his opponent. Sullivan was a battering ram. He pummeled Kilrain round after round. Had Jake stayed with his skill and stayed away from the lunging Sullivan, he might very well have prevailed in the contest. Alas, Jake stood toe to toe with Sullivan and absorbed the punishment. The early rounds, the first thirty or so, saw a fair test of the fighters' respective talents. Jake gave as good as he got in the early going. Got up the hopes of some in his corner, including me; I'd bet a bundle on him. Back and forth, round after round, rock-hard blow after rock-hard blow it went. Kilrain had a good cut man in his corner; he needed one.

As the fight wore on, the intense heat sapped the strength of both fighters. Kilrain resorted to frequent flops to the canvas as a survival strategy. Sullivan, bull that he was, couldn't finish him. In truth, after the fortieth round, neither man landed a blow of consequence. Kilrain survived the last half hour or so owing to the fact Sullivan had nothing left with which to finish the man. At the seventy-fifth respite, one of Kilrain's corner men approached Sullivan's corner with an offer. Kilrain would concede the fight, if Sullivan conceded the in-ring bet. With the signal to return for round seventy-six, Kilrain stood in his corner. Sullivan never left his stool. Inexplicably Jake's second corner man threw a sponge in the ring, ending the fight in favor of Sullivan.

Sullivan retained his crown at the pinnacle of his career in what was to be the last bare-knuckle fight. Probably good it was; those bare-knuckle brawls were brutal. They produced more broken bones and cuts than imaginable. Facial cuts bleed profusely. By the latter stages of the fight, Kilrain resembled one of those painted Comanche warriors at Adobe Walls. I've a strong stomach where such things are concerned, but that day I saw through the thin curtain of sport into the eyes of barbarism beyond. I'd never admit as much to a reformer, but I saw it. Putting on gloves, limiting the number of rounds, and admitting a judged decision all seemed prudent restraints to preserve the fate of the sport.

Kilrain didn't absorb all the damage that day. I lost my worldly fortune on the fight. Emma, never one to ask after our finances, noticed the crimp in our lifestyle while I got our fortunes back on their feet. You'd think a man would learn a lesson from an experience like that, but such is not the case with a true sport. The excitement you find at the edge of risk is habit forming after the fashion of vices like tobacco and whiskey. I had a well-developed appetite by then. Had it most of my life.

I found myself once more adrift in reflection. I could now observe how my hunger for urgent gratification changed over the years. Back in the day, I got it from the thrill of the hunt in hostile territory. Next came imposing my will to enforce the law in rough circumstances. The edge of physical danger moved on to the excitement of risk at the gaming tables. Boxing took over when reformers foreclosed on gaming enjoyment. I still feel the thrill of the contest, but I see now how my appetite has mellowed. The passage of time cannot be denied when it comes to a young man's adventures. I admit my age, if only to myself. Where did it go? Ephemeral youth, unappreciated by those who have it, until one day dawns to the realization: it's gone.

CHAPTER TWENTY-SIX

Shanley's Grill
Forty-Third and Broadway

"Remarkable story," Runyon said. "You don't hear it that way in Sullivan's biographies and news accounts. I believe he described the seventy-fifth round as viciously fought with Kilrain beaten to a pulp against the ropes."

"I seem to recall reading that bit of balderdash. To this day, I say if Jake's corner man hadn't thrown in the sponge, Kilrain would have won the fight and taken the title."

"Would have changed the fight game's future."

"Would, given the rest of Sullivan's record — five- and six-round exhibitions with overmatched middle-weights, most of whom couldn't punch their way out of wet newspaper. I doubt we'd have heard of him again."

"A distorted historical record to be sure. How was the shepherd's pie?"

I returned to the moment. "Warm to the cockles of a man's heart on a cold winter day."

"Cockles with the soul of a poet."

A glare warned him away from such talk.

"Your secret is safe with me. Well, probably with Emma, too. She's a remarkable woman to put up with the likes of you and your chosen pursuits. I can't think there are many women who would."

"That's been my experience. More than that, Emma was always ready for anything, likely why I'd been enchanted from the moment I met her. She even took to boxing when I did, or tried to."

"Tried to?"

"Emma accompanied me to New Orleans in '91 for the middle-weight title fight between Jack Dempsey and Bob Fitzsimmons. She had a genuine enthusiasm for the fight game. She was bound, bent, and determined to see the fight in spite of the fact the fair sex was barred from pugilistic contests at the time. She bristled at the notion the spectacle might be too violent for her gentle sensibilities to observe. Emma wouldn't hold with any taboo she deemed dismissive of women. Never did. My interest in the sport contributed to her attraction to it, but I believe her determination to attend the fight was born of her disdain for Victorian prohibitions. There's that word again. Such an attitude might have appeared improper to most in those days, certainly stuffy society matrons, who populate the ranks of the reform minded. Probably most sporting men, too, preferred the manly art be reserved as a manly pursuit. Not me; I found her stubborn resistance to convention quite charming. Notwithstanding, history indeed repeats itself."

"Did she manage it?"

"Manage it?"

"Attending the fight."

"After a fashion. She dressed as a man to sneak past security. They spotted her, of course, and arrested her."

"Arrested her in your company?"

"Indeed. I'm quite sure the poor constable had no idea what he was getting into. Emma was furious, spouting insults and invective as they carted her away."

"You rescued her, of course."

"Of course. After the fight."

"You let her sit in gaol while you attended the fight?"

"She knew the risks. She made her own decision. I had a rather substantial bet in play. Besides, I found her temporary discomfort somewhat amusing. I assured her later the small delay in her release afforded her an opportunity to impress the injustice of her predicament upon the arresting authorities."

"I can imagine you caught an earful for that."

"Actually, she was quite appreciative when I bailed her out."

"I should think she'd have felt abandoned."

"No fear of that. I simply directed her ire toward archaic strictures on the rights of women. Then, too, there was the bright side."

"Bright side?"

"I'd won my bet."

"Did she ever attempt it again?"

"She returned to New Orleans with me the following year for the title fight between John L. Sullivan and Gentleman Jim Corbett. This time she left fight attendance to me."

New Orleans
September 7, 1892
John L. Sullivan signed on to a title bout with up and comer Gentleman Jim Corbett. The fight took place at the Pelican Athletic

Club. Sullivan had the title, the reputation, and a cultivated image of invincibility — all the ingredients needed to run up the odds in his favor. I liked Corbett. He was quick with his hands and fast on his feet. Sullivan was a little thicker than I'd seen him in his last fight. Like me, he'd racked up a few birthdays since then. While he was younger than me, I remembered the onset of those years. Having learned nothing from the Kilrain fight, I bet it all on the challenger. I could feel cracks in the champ's armor deep down in my gut.

Old John L. stayed with the kid for twenty-one rounds, but he couldn't land the kind of punishment he laid on Jake Kilrain. The kid danced, circled, jabbed, and counter-punched when the champ's feet got heavy late in a round. As the rounds wore on, those feet got heavy earlier and earlier. Sullivan got frustrated, unable to do much damage, let alone put the kid away. He got aggressive. Opened himself up. Corbett pounced, again and again.

Somewhere around the fifteenth, I figured the kid had him; it was only a matter of time and circumstance. I stood to make a bountiful take, but I confess I watched with a certain melancholy. Not that I had a great deal of admiration for Sullivan as a fighter, but it was nevertheless the end of an era of sorts. It brought me mindful of those heydays in Dodge and all my pals. We'd been at the top of our game back then, just like old John L. Time has a way of catching up with all of us. It caught up with Sullivan that night in the form of a vicious right cross that sent him to the canvas for the count, his title, and his career.

Watching the champ lie still on the canvas was painful. I'd called the fight; I'd won a bundle. I should have been slapping my palm with the program and lighting up a perfecto. Instead, visions of John L.'s past glories mingled with memories of old pals and triumphs gone by. Billy Dixon, Bill Tilghman, Ben Thompson, even Doc Holliday — heaven knows why — along with some others whose faces I couldn't quite make out. They were all there. Standing around the ring like it might be a wake for the late, great John L. Sullivan. He was one of the best brawlers the fight game had ever produced, and now it was over. There we stood with him. Some of the most competent men to have traveled and tamed the West, and we were done, too. For most, all that was left was a memory. *Memories . . .*

"Bat, you all right?"

Runyon hauled me back from that reverie. "All right? Sure, sure."

"It must have been one hell of a fight."

I met his gaze, still a little far off in my eye. "It was. Sullivan was one of a kind. It all has to end sometime. You know it in your head. You're just never ready for it in your heart."

"He was a fighter. It happens."

"It does. I just saw a lot of . . . I don't know, life in that moment. Life gone by."

"Well, you still had your winnings."

"I did. Then Corbett put the title on the line two years later."

"How did that go?"

Jacksonville, Florida
January 25, 1894

The title bout matched top contender Charlie Mitchell against the champ, Gentleman Jim Corbett, for a purse of twenty thousand dollars. Mitchell was a fine fighter. I knew him and liked the Englishman. After I watched him work out, I worried he'd trained down from two hundred pounds to one hundred sixty for the bout. The measurables — reach, weight, and so on —

247

favored Corbett, a fact that became apparent to the odds-makers.

The betting line favored Corbett from the open. The odds continued to build as the fight approached, the bookmaker premium growing rich to attract action to the match. At three to one, I was drawn in by chance and my affection for my English friend. Chance got the better of me when Corbett put Charlie away in three rounds. In hindsight I should have seen the game getting the better of judgment. With cards there were fifty-two in the deck; odds could be calculated. With fighters, the possibilities were limitless, and, as such, risk could be wildly unpredictable. You think you know the game; you make a judgment call. The odds pull you in, but it's not really a matter of chance. The fighters are human with human capacities for good days and bad. You can't always see those coming; that's where the game beats you.

Then there entered the prospect for mischief. As the purses and promises of titles grew, so did temptations to the principals involved. The sport might turn on far more than chance. If you could find a square match, the odds tempted a man and fogged his judgment. Whilst I didn't suspect the fix was in on the Corbett and Mitchell bout, once again, I'd been seduced by the possibility of outsized gain, however improbable. Knowledge and critical thinking departed the scene. I'd flattened my bundle on the odds-maker's altar and the tug of my own sentiment.

CHAPTER TWENTY-SEVEN

Lundy's Delicatessen
Broadway, New York

I couldn't believe I'd let myself get talked into this again. It could only have been a weak moment. I waded through the lunch-hour throng to the counter and ordered pastrami on rye. It came with a dollop of white stuff that looked suspiciously like potato salad and a chunky dill pickle some rabbi declared edible. I found a recently vacated booth with a busboy clearing away leavings of the last diner's lunch. What on earth Runyon found so inviting about the place continued to elude me. I took my seat. The busboy delivered a glass of water.

Runyon arrived to run the counter gauntlet. He found his way to the booth, juggling his usual coffee along with a plate bearing two half sandwiches. Two half sandwiches on wheat. I inspected them curiously.

"Half tuna salad, half egg salad," he said.

"Couldn't make up your mind?"

"My favorites." He shrugged.

"Clearly some deficiency of the taste buds."

"You have it your way, and I'll have it mine. I chose the place in deference to the depleted financial condition in which we last left you."

"That was two decades ago. My circumstances have improved some since then."

"To be sure, but at the time I suspect you weren't a knight of the Metropole round-table."

"No, I suppose not, though my pecuniary embarrassment didn't last long."

"Cashed out another fortuitous bet?"

"Not exactly. I got my first taste of this town."

New York
May 1895

As luck would have it, soon after the Corbett-Mitchell fight, fortune flashed her bright smile upon me with an opportunity to right the underpinnings of financial stability. George Gould, a man unknown to me, became the subject of mortal threats against his life. Heir to the fortune of railroad financier Jay Gould, the progeny, it appeared, had also fallen heir to the animas of one or more victims of the ruthless methods his father used in amassing his empire. A friend of New York City police commissioner Theodore Roosevelt, Gould turned to a man expert in such matters for advice. T.R. suggested the services of a bodyguard, preferably one whose notoriety would send a message to those behind the threats. He directed superintendent of New York police, Thomas Byrnes, to solicit my interest in securing Mr. Gould's continued good health. And so, with prospects at the time being somewhat meager, I entrained for New York and my first bite at the Big Apple.

New York is like a beautiful whore. Most of them aren't; this one was. She seduced me from the moment I stepped off the train. Sprawling, muscular, fast moving, never stopping, she beat with a sophisticated verve all her own. The job proved icing on the cake of her charms. Living in a mansion and circulating among the upper crust of the country's upper crust proved a heady brew. The social swirl surrounding Gould sent us to parties, galas, and sporting diversions from the track to deep-sea fishing — things of which a buffalo hunter, plainsman, frontier lawman, and gambler knew nothing. Well, not entirely; I knew horseflesh and had some appreciation of odds at the track and in the ring. Mr. Gould found the latter entertaining insights added to the cache of my reputation.

The threats on George Gould's person were real enough, but the coward responsible had no conviction to act on them. Nonetheless, I remained vigilant when circumstances called for it and thoroughly enjoyed myself when given leave to do so. George turned out to be a charming companion as much taken with my celebrity as my part in protecting him. He took great pleasure in showing me off to his many friends, taking added stature from being escorted by the renowned W. B. Masterson. I let him bask in it if it pleased him. Ponied up a yarn or two to help his cause along. At the stipend he paid me, it was a small price, and likely the ensuing gossip added a protective layer to my client's safety.

The long blue arm of T.R.'s police force caught up with the culprit behind the threats later that year. Shortly thereafter I was bundled onto a private railcar with good wishes, a handsome bonus, and first-class service along my return trip to Denver.

"Roosevelt himself recommended you?"

"He did."

"By reputation?"

"By acquaintance."

"You knew him before New York?"

"We met briefly during his ranching years in Dakota."

"You must have made an impression on him."

"I had that effect on some people."

"And so, you were smitten by the charms of our fair city."

"I was, though I wasn't quite through with the West just yet, or perhaps the West wasn't then through with me."

"So you went back to Denver."

"I did. Though, I must confess, Denver seemed rather dowdy by New York standards. It did offer one small advantage. It took less money to prosper on the front range than it did to mine the stone canyons in Gotham. That's where boxing once again grasped at my appetite for risk and the inevitable connection it breeds to my wallet."

Following the Mitchell fight, Gentleman Jim retired his title undefeated. A hastily conceived bout between a pair of Mics, Peter Maher and Steve O'Donnell, handed Maher the title before O'Donnell's gloves were laced tight. Maher's claim on the title seemed tenuous at best. A Texas sport named Stuart saw opportunity there and signed Maher to fight Bob Fitzsimmons in what could be billed as an authentic title fight, Fitzsimmons having previously defeated Maher.

I eagerly joined the sports gathering in El Paso. The promoter had hired Pinkerton to provide security services. William Pinkerton retained me to head his security detail. This assured my expenses and an income, allowing me to consider my wagering opportunities.

By reputation, I liked Maher's chances. After watching both fighters spar, my opinion wavered. The prospects, it seemed, stacked up evenly in the flesh. From there it became a matter of weighing the odds.

The match turned into a lightning rod for reformers on both sides of the border. The religious class nattered the Texas governor's office until the governor ordered a company of Texas Rangers to El Paso to assure the match was not fought on that state's hallowed ground. Mexican authorities were similarly harassed until they dispatched troops to Juarez to prevent the event from crossing the border into her sovereign territory. Thus, we found ourselves stymied by a dearth of hospitality. As chief of security and, in part, I suspect, for my notoriety, I found myself the brunt of ranger pressure. I wanted no part of tangling with a pack of quasi-military thugs. Thankfully, an unlikely sponsor came through with a stratagem to break the standoff.

Our breakthrough came at the invitation of Judge Roy Bean, self-proclaimed law west of the Pecos. He invited, and the fight moved to Langtry, Texas, site of an island in the midst of the Rio Grande. The island being neither in Texas nor Mexico. Inspired really, though not entirely, out of the goodness of the hanging judge's heart.

We loaded the whole show, rangers and all, on a west-bound train to Langtry. There a ring was erected on the island where the bout could be staged. The method to Judge Bean's magnanimous gesture soon became apparent. The island was served by a rope bridge from the shore. The bridge sprouted a toll for those wishing to cross for the fight.

The rangers opted not to cross, perhaps thinking the island beyond their jurisdiction. They contented themselves to watch the bout from the shore.

By fight time, the odds drew me into Maher's corner. The odds-makers had the right of it; Fitz made short work of Maher. You'd suppose by then I should have realized odds that trump an even physical match seduce good judgment. You'd suppose that, but then you'd miss the elixir of risk. Thanks to Bill Pinkerton, I had fare left to go home.

Lundy's Delicatessen
Broadway, New York
"Odds again," Runyon said.

"They're like that come-hither look in a beautiful woman's eye. Cupidity, greed . . . neither one is good for clear thinking."

"I can see that. I suppose those same odds can tug at all manner of sports besides gamblers."

"What do you mean?"

"You know. You hear stories. Fighters, corner men, referees . . ."

"You're talking about the Sharkey-Fitzsimmons fight."

"One example."

"Maybe. Maybe it was, and maybe it wasn't. But I'll tell you one thing sure: Wyatt

257

had no part in it."

"What makes you so certain?"

"I know the man."

Runyon glanced at his watch. "Have to get back to the salt mine. Drinks at the Metropole?"

"You don't drink."

"You do."

"If I must."

CHAPTER TWENTY-EIGHT

December 1896

"Sailor Tom" Sharkey signed to fight Robert "Ruby" Fitzsimmons for his heavyweight title at Mechanics Arena in San Francisco. The Maher fight had painfully purchased my respect for Fitzsimmons as a fighter. I didn't think much of Sharkey. I knew Wyatt had befriended the man, coached him some, and had squired him around some bouts. I didn't hold that against either of them. I just thought Fitz would have the better of a square fight. I couldn't attend, but I put a few dead presidents on the Ruby with my Denver book.

As it turned out, Wyatt got the call to referee the fight. The whole affair came off star-crossed from the beginning. Wyatt entered the ring heeled. Why, heaven only knows. Maybe he felt he needed protection. More likely he forgot he was packing. Those things become second nature to some of us.

The police security detail didn't see it that way, of course, and, much to his humiliation, Wyatt was forced to disarm ringside for all to see.

The fight commenced, evenly matched through the early rounds by the accounts I read. Somewhat surprising really, as I expected better from Fitzsimmons. Trouble reared its ugly head in the eighth when Fitz caught Sharkey with what Wyatt saw as a low blow. He ruled foul and awarded the fight to Sharkey. The crowd went wild, not having seen the offense as Wyatt did. A postfight examination revealed Sharkey bore the mark of a blow well below the belt. It did nothing to silence those who argued Wyatt had been paid to fix the fight. The sharps with money on Fitzsimmons argued a mark like Sharkey's might be induced by an injection of iodine. Who would know such a thing more than one capable of similar subterfuge?

Nothing would satisfy the aggrieved. I defended Wyatt at the time and continue to do so to this very day. It was all to no avail. Wyatt took a painful loss to his reputation and I another painful loss to my wallet.

"After all of that you remain convinced Wyatt Earp had no hand in fixing the fight?"

"I know he didn't."

"Did he tell you that?"

"No. Didn't need to."

"He didn't need to."

"Of course not. I know Wyatt Earp. He's a man of character. I've entrusted my life to his hands countless times. I dare say, I know him better than the younger of his brothers. He simply wouldn't do such a thing."

"Title fight money can be tempting."

"Not to Wyatt Earp."

"Even if no one found out?"

"Wouldn't matter."

"Why not?"

"Wyatt would know. Nobody holds Wyatt Earp to a higher standard than Wyatt Earp. He would have known; that's all I need to know."

"Remarkable."

"What's remarkable about that?"

"Your friendship. For that, I shall take your word for it."

I signaled the bartender for a second Manhattan. Runyon got his coffee freshened in the bargain and lit a cigarette.

"I remember the first time I saw you," he

261

said through a cloud of smoke. "It was in Pueblo. I was just a kid. You and Mr. Floto promoted a fight between Flynn and some Mex. Flynn beat the Mex like a drum. Then I watched you pay off the fighters with deputy sheriff's badges from Tombstone. You claimed to have worn them at the O.K. Corral. They both settled for the badges."

"Sentimental souvenirs."

"Two of them?"

"Receipts were slim that night."

"I don't recall ever hearing you were even at the O.K. Corral."

"I wasn't."

"Then how do you explain the badges?"

"Sentimental souvenirs." With that I had to laugh at the memory.

"What's so funny?"

"Sheriff's badges. If I had been there, I'd have been with Wyatt, his brothers, and Doc. Johnny Behan was sheriff. He backed the McLaurys and Clantons."

"So you pulled the wool over a couple of dumb fighters. It wasn't quite so easy with Mr. Floto. As I recall you two about came to blows over the split."

"You mean Denver Fats? Your 'Mr. Floto' couldn't have fought his way out of a cheap whorehouse. You did work for him, didn't you?"

"That came later, back in my drinking days."

"Youthful indiscretion. I shall overlook it on account of my own failure in judgment."

"How's that?"

"A man so crooked, he couldn't lay straight in bed, and I missed it."

"That is crooked."

Denver
1898

I knew Otto Floto. If you followed professional prize fighting in those days you got to know most of the regular sports. Floto and I both hung our hats in Denver, so we were better acquainted than most. In what turned out to be a weak moment, I got into a discussion with him over the fact Denver had no venue with which to draw prize fights to town. We discussed the possibility of establishing our own pugilistic club from which to promote matches. We shopped the idea around to a few potential financial backers and got an enthusiastic reception to the prospect. Floto was a sports stringer for *The Denver Post* at the time. His bosses thought quite highly of the enterprise. We talked up the idea with two of the better known fighters in town, Kid McCoy and Reddy Gallagher. Both agreed to fight out of the proposed Colorado Athletic Club. Things looked promising, until Floto showed his true greedy colors.

We found a building to house the club, and Floto undertook arrangements to acquire use of it. About that time McCoy got seduced away to greener pastures in the East, where he involved himself in some of the shadiest fights ever fixed. We might have bid him good riddance had we known at the time. When arrangements for the club facility were finalized, Otto Floto emerged as sole proprietor. He decided our idea was his. With his column and financial backers at the *Post,* he figured he had all the clout he needed to promote his fight cards, without cutting me in for any of it.

I was furious, as you might imagine. Good thing for the fat man I'd mellowed by those years. Time was I would have called him out for pulling a stunt like that. I never could abide duplicity of any description. "Don't get mad," Emma said. "Get even." Emma could always be counted on to put a common sense point on misfortune.

In early '99 I formed the Olympic Athletic Club to promote rival exhibitions. I found an abandoned music theater on Sixteenth Street that would prove serviceable to my purposes with modest renovation. By July we were ready to take on the Otto-man's empire.

Floto had it all figured out, except for one little detail: I could draw fighters he couldn't on the strength of my reputation. He did have one lever at his disposal that I lacked: his column at the *Post* afforded a powerful promotional tool. I'd taken up my pen against reformers in letters to editors and proven I could go toe to toe with the best of them in pot and ink. Floto's scribblings were about as inspired and insightful as a lummox so dumb he couldn't get the pee out of his boot if the directions were on the heel. To even the score I talked myself onto *George's Weekly* as sports editor. *George's* lacked the circulation of the *Post,* but my reputation brought a cachet to the sheet sure to benefit both our causes. It gave me leave to scald Floto's follies at every opportunity, and the fat man presented no shortage of opportunities.

Reformers greeted the prospect of sanctioned prize fighting in Denver with an ordinance against it. I'd seen this scam before. It reminded me of the gambling prohibitions I'd so often encountered in my Dodge City and later boom-town days. His Otto-ship got around the boxing prohibition by staging legal "sparring contests." A

man couldn't bet on dancing partners —
there was no sport in it. I was thrilled. The
bloated fop had set the kettle to boil for his
own goose without thinking another thing
of it. I pounced with a *George's Weekly*
column, mocking the Colorado Club's farci-
cal imitation of a boxing match. I suggested
the club's canvas ring might be more enter-
tainingly employed by a ballet exhibition.

The following week the Olympic Club announced a pugilistic bout between two well-
known fighters at the time. The match
would be fought to a decision. We chal-
lenged the Denver ordinance in court, paid
our fine in advance, and obtained an injunc-
tion suspending enforcement until our suit
might be adjudicated. Floto cried foul in
the *Post,* but, his protestations aside, the
way was paved for my fight to proceed.

The fighters turned in a fine match,
received to a raucous packed house and a
balanced book of wagers. The Olympic
Club was a hit and the enterprise off to a
promising start. I, of course, reviewed the
fight in glowing detail for *George's Weekly,*
in response to which Floto could only add
the sourest of grapes.

Things went well for a year and more, but,
with the passage of time, his Otto-ship and
the bully megaphone at the *Post* began to

take its toll. When Floto persuaded Gallagher to cross over to his side, the air in Denver began to grow foul. Floto and Gallagher cut the prices for their exhibitions to the point it became difficult to raise a purse sufficient to attract top talent to the ring in Denver. My *George's Weekly* column flogged the watered broth served at the Colorado Club. True sports nodded their approval of my editorial views, but patrons paying paltry prices it seemed were more easily amused. I began to grow weary of Denver's tepid prospects.

The Floto-Gallagher confrontations became more vitriolic. Gasbag Otto and I came to blows over a chance encounter on the street. He fled like a stuck javelina when I took my cane to him. Soon after, rumors of an assassination plot against me, attributed to Gallagher, began to circulate. They troubled Emma; I wasn't much bothered. When confronted with the fact I knew of his intentions, Gallagher's gunman decamped for parts unknown, and Gallagher himself disavowed any knowledge of what he called "spurious rumor."

The last cloud gathered with the threat of reformers darkening the horizon. Grifters and hypocrites insinuated themselves into positions of power, allowing them to cow people into all manner of tight-laced social oppression. Denver donned herself in all the elegance of an outhouse cotillion. I counted it time to pull up stakes and leave thin mountain air to those with an appetite for it.

CHAPTER TWENTY-NINE

A week went by before I next saw Runyon. He stopped in at the office on a Thursday morning to suggest we have dinner at Shanley's that evening before covering a contender card at Madison Square Garden. A good steak and entertaining conversation seemed likely to offer more entertainment than a fight card of unknowns trying to work their way into legitimate contention. Still, one never knew when a fighter of note might emerge on the boxing scene. I confess there is an element of discovery for a fight analyst when witness to so rare an occurrence. The possibility adds an element of anticipation to an exhibition that more than likely will end in jaded mediocrity.

As usual I arrived in time to secure a table and order a drink before Runyon made his signature harried appearance.

"Sorry I'm late. Busy day. Looks like I might sell a story for a Broadway play."

"Congratulations."

He held up a hand. "Not yet. We're in the talking stage. Script concepts. Time enough to celebrate when we've a check in hand."

"How about 'good luck' then?"

"Always accepted. Anything on tonight's card look interesting?"

I shook my head. "Dinner."

We ordered our usual steaks, Caesar salads, and potatoes fried with onions.

"Let's see, when we last left you, you were planning to leave Denver. What brought you to New York?"

"At the time, I thought money. Turned out it was fortune . . . good fortune, that is."

New York
June 1902
I'd had my fill of the West, or so I thought at the time. Sporting action was drying up with all the reformers harping on righteous morality. Emma was worn out with worry by Denver. She thought it only a matter of time before Floto or Gallagher conjured up another attempt on my life. If I had a nickel for every one of those I've faced . . . Never mind.

We thought about California some. Wyatt and Josephine seemed to like it well enough.

Heydays in the West were over. I'd gotten a taste of New York while playing bodyguard to Mr. Gould. Rubbing elbows with the city's upper crust convinced me there was money to be made in New York. I hadn't any particular skills suited to it (or so I thought at the time), but I had a reputation I could trade on. Something would turn up. It always did. If you don't go west, you go east.

We started east with a visit to Chicago. I had some sporting friends there and, of course, Bill Pinkerton. Action on the sporting scene was light and riskier than the luck of the draw, courtesy of the long blue arm of the law. Pinkerton tried to convince me to go to work for him again. I'd done a little work for him once or twice, but the life of a gumshoe private dick no longer held any romance for me. My heart was in the boxing ring. The best of that action could be found in New York. Emma and I continued on to the cobbled canyons of Gotham and a new life amid the civilized amenities of modern society.

We arrived in New York and found our way to Longacre Square. It may have been the glow emerging from those new-fangled electric lights on Broadway that drew us in. We settled into a small apartment and took in the city together. It didn't take long for Emma to fall in love with New York. City life suited her. She'd shake her head and wonder at how long we'd contented ourselves with the meager amenities available on the Western frontier. I must admit I grew comfortable with it, too. The West had been good to me. I thrived on it as a young man and fondly remember those days. You can take a man out of the West, I suppose, but you can't take the West out of a man. As true as that sentiment might be, the West remained where it belonged for a man my age, firmly ensconced in fond memory.

New York fit us like a comfortable shoe. The next order of business became finding a livelihood. The fight scene offered opportunities to referee, lend my name to promotion, and hold the stakes when they were high or in need of special security. The first opportunity to present itself was offered by a fight promoter who thought my reputation might play well in his plan to promote New York boxing in England. Emma thought the idea of visiting England a once in a lifetime experience. With encouragement such as that I agreed to the enterprise. As luck would have it, I missed the boat.

I didn't mean to miss the boat, but soon

after our arrival in New York I found myself incarcerated. An allegation was put forward that I'd run a crooked faro game. The situation did not improve when the arresting officer found me carrying a gun. By the time I cleared myself, the English promotion ship had sailed.

Between pugilistic events I could always find opportunity at the track to match a man with his wits. I'd always been a fair judge of horseflesh. Raceways afforded the opportunity to put that eye to profitable endeavor. And so it was, in no more than the blink of an eye, 1902 turned into 1903, and an opportunity came along that would take my life off on a comfortable path to new purpose.

I first met young Bill Lewis in Kansas. He was a cub reporter for *The New York Sun* at the time. The paper sent him West on assignment to stir up colorful Western stories. His brother, Alfred, was a cowhand with a hidden head for writing. Bill thought my reputation worth a story or two. I obliged; seemed like it couldn't do any harm. Al tagged along for the listen. I suppose I owe some of my unearned reputation to telling those stories. Al later turned a few of them into novels about a Bat Masterson I didn't recognize. Bill's stories in *The Sun* toed closer to the taper of truth, but put me in a fine light all the same. They were out around the time Fry and I exchanged pencil whippings in the Ford County dailies. Later Bill followed my sports columns in *George's Weekly.* He got the idea I could write. My reputation didn't hurt the byline, either.

In 1903 Bill became managing editor of *The Morning Telegraph* and offered me a position as sports writer. I was fifty years old. I loved boxing. To me that was sport. Sports writing sounded like a comfortable pair of slippers. *The Telegraph,* too, felt like a fine fit. It catered to a carriage-trade clientele whose interests ran to the finer pursuits of life. The paper covered the social scene, theater, and sporting events like no other sheet in town. You could also have a little fun with lurid tabloid scandal fodder or sample your favorite crime and corruption with smidgeons of lascivious titillation. The upper crust enjoyed the seamy undersides of the city from afar. They paid for it, too — five cents, where the other dailies charged three. It didn't matter to the privileged class who made up our circulation.

The offices were housed in a converted streetcar stable. I always found a chuckle's worth of irony in the hoi polloi getting their latest scoop from a joint formerly given to a different kind of scoop. Be that as it may, the newsroom was every bit as entertaining as some of the gambling halls I'd frequented over the years. You could find a poker game day or night. Chorus girls and sports hung out with the news hounds, hoping, I suppose, to ingratiate themselves into some sort of notoriety.

The Telegraph was a great fit for me. I got paid to follow sports and pen a few lines of analysis or opinion, commodities of which I am seldom in short supply. Too good to be true, really. Larceny could scarcely have been more rewarding and with no fear of incarceration. My columns absorbed my affections for and experience in boxing. I seldom wandered into other sporting territories such as racing, baseball, or the abominable practice of football. I might, on occasion, stray into subjects of interest or vexation, should I have something to say. I seldom did in my early years, though, more recently, I've not been hesitant to vent common sense when confronted by some misbegotten societal abomination. We came to call those columns Masterson's Views on Timely Topics. More often than not, those musings are drawn to politics, patriotism, and so-called reform provocations.

I felt quite at home at the *Telegraph.* Our

editorial bent made no secret of our distaste for incursions by reformers into the mainstreams of society. I'd developed a taste for dipping a venomous pen in ink where political humbugs, self-righteous moralists, and purveyors of tedious ill-humor asserted themselves in matters where personal liberty or jocularity ought to prevail.

Shanley's
Forty-Third and Broadway
Fresh-baked apple pie topped off the meal in time to hail a cab to the Garden. We clattered along the cobbles to the pitch and sway of the coach.

"It makes for quite a story. Buffalo hunter to lawman to gambler to sportswriter," Runyon said.

"You make it sound finished."

"I don't mean to. It's only so . . . so improbable."

"Improbable? Oh, I don't know; one thing just sort of led to another."

"Who would ever have charted such a course?"

The question gave me pause to reflect. Only one answer came to me at length.

"Bat Masterson, I guess."

"So he did."

"There's more, of course."

276

"Of course. What next?"

I thought for a bit. Indeed, what next? I smiled at a memory. Another friend.

"T.R."

CHAPTER THIRTY

Morning Telegraph

Runyon showed up for lunch unannounced one rainy noon with spring threatening to break the bonds of winter. He had a paper bag of sandwiches from that place he liked. Pastrami for me, that vial smelling egg salad for him. He counted on *The Telegraph* to have coffee. We had our dish-water excuse and ate at my desk.

"I listen to your stories of the West and understand why you and President Roosevelt got on so well. It is plenty clear why he would want to appoint you a U.S. marshal. When did you meet him?"

I had to think.

"We first met during his ranching days in Dakota Territory, not long after he established the second ranch. Elkhorn, I think he called it. The first one, the Maltese Cross, opened in '84, so I make it around fall of '85. We did a little hunting. He loved to hunt. The bigger and wilder the game the better; that's the way it was with him. The West bred hardy men who could take care of themselves in rugged circumstances. He admired that. No doubt because he had plenty of flint to go with his steel. We met in passing. He didn't stay in the West long after that year. You no doubt had more congress with him in Cuba than I did back then.

"McKinley's death was a despicable act of anarchist cowardice. Such vermin are capable of little else. I, for one, counted us fortunate to have a man of T.R.'s timbre to succeed him. In Roosevelt we had a man of character. A leader of men. Courageous, rugged, hardy like the country he served. He might have been bred of New York privilege, but he could hold his own in the West. Some might have taken him for a tenderfoot, but there was nothing tender about the man. He relished a contest. Hunted the harshest conditions. Proved himself on the battlefield, as you know. He knew the fight game and loved it near as much as I do. I was proud to call him friend before either of us ever set foot in that gilded cage they call the White House."

"Is that the first time he offered you a marshal's appointment?"

I nodded. "Wanted me to go to Arkansas and clean up the Oklahoma nations. He thought I'd be 'Just the man for the job,' is how he put it." I could almost feel the firm clap on the shoulder that went with the offer. It came with that beaver-tooth grin of his, too.

"He was right, of course. Why did you turn him down?"

"I'd have caused more trouble than I could ever have cleaned up. The nations were wide open and lawless in those days. Reservation Indians weren't so much the problem; it was the outlaw haven the nations had become. I knew full well who was out there. Not by name, mind you, but I knew the type. I knew I'd attract them, too. Every dime-novel, starstruck kid with a gun and an appetite for notoriety would have found me an inviting target. I told T.R. I didn't need any more killings to my credit."

"But you've said your reputation was somewhat exaggerated."

"It was, but nobody knew that. Exaggerated or not, it was there."

"So, he honored your preferences."

"Sure. What else was he going to do?"

"He was the president and a man who could be downright persuasive even when he wasn't president."

"I told him he'd be better served by the likes of Bill Tilghman and Bass Reeves. Besides, I had a good excuse. Law and order is a good excuse where such appointments are concerned."

"It was an excuse?"

I glanced around so as to be sure no one might overhear. "It was. I had no interest in returning to life in the West. I'm a Broadway guy now. I like New York just fine. T.R. more than anyone should have understood that."

"And that's why you accepted the New York deputy's shield in '05."

I smiled at the recollection. "That and two thousand a year for doing nothing. I was assigned to security for a grand jury that almost never went into session. My duties consisted of stopping by the office on payday to pick up my check."

"Nice work if you can get it."

"It was, until T.R. left office."

"I'm sure it afforded the opportunity to go about town legally healed."

I felt the familiar heavy presence in my coat pocket. My gaze narrowed to a knowing half squint. "It did."

"Until T.R. left office."

"Old Taft might have been T.R.'s pick to succeed him, but the man was less enamored of an old gunfighter's reputation than efficient government. Can't say I blamed him for that. We had a nice run while it lasted. Don't think for a moment I was disarmed by the loss of my appointment, however. I'm always healed."

"I'm still surprised you were able to turn the president down when he offered you the Oklahoma appointment. He wasn't a man to take no for an answer."

"No, he was not. Like the time he invited me to a black-tie dinner at the White House. Shortly before he left office he threw a dinner for senior army and navy brass. I happened to be in Washington at the time. T.R. held the military in high regard. We both did. He thought I'd enjoy the evening, and the flag ranks would enjoy the novelty of my presence. I had no appetite for it, though. A rough cob like me didn't belong in such distinguished company. I'd never have found my way to the White House in a million years if it hadn't been for my friendship with T.R.

"When I attempted to decline, he insisted. You couldn't simply say no to him, so I did the only thing a man could do in that position."

"What was that?"

"I lied. Well, not exactly lied; I told him I'd consider it. I knew in my heart I wouldn't attend. I told myself I did it to give him the satisfaction of my ascent. They went so far as to find a suit of formal wear to fit me. I found it laid out in my hotel room when I returned that afternoon. I made a feeble attempt to put the horse collar on, but I just couldn't do it. I didn't have the heart to tell the president no. I sent him a telegram and caught the next train north."

CHAPTER THIRTY-ONE

Metropole Hotel
Forty-Second and Broadway

We next met for drinks the following Friday after work. Walking up Broadway, I hunched into the warmth of my coat, winter chill more noticeable having been teased by the prospect of spring. The Metropole provided warmth and relief. I took a booth and ordered a Manhattan, while awaiting Runyon's arrival. He showed up right behind the waiter delivering my drink. He ordered his coffee.

"Don't like the cold," he said.

"Can't last much longer."

"Yes it can. Lasted too long already."

"Go south."

He glanced around at the five o'clock crowd with an expressive gleam in his eye. "And give up all this? I can't bear the thought of being cut off from the action."

"Yes, well then I suggest you make peace

with the cold. Nature shall indeed have her way."

"You wax philosophical this evening." He tapped a cigarette from a fresh pack and lit up. He exhaled a stream of blue smoke. "You wrote a series of magazine articles about your friends for Alfred Lewis a few years ago."

"Aught seven," I recalled.

"Any tidbits from those articles we haven't heard yet?"

"Sure. We've discussed my story and the parts my friends played. The articles were about their stories. I've always thought their stories more interesting than min, anyway. I merely had the good fortune to be present for some of each of their stories."

"So, what don't we know about Bill Tilghman?"

I drifted off on the question.

Bill Tilghman
Bill did some ranching near Dodge after our buffalo hunting days. He was elected Dodge City marshal in '84, launching what would become a distinguished career as a lawman. Bill was cool headed, fearless, and a competent man packing a badge. Eventually that led to a U.S. marshal's appointment in Oklahoma Territory, the one T.R.

once spoke to me about.

The nations, as Indian reservation lands in Oklahoma Territory came to be known, became lawless lands and a haven for all manner of outlaws, killers, and cutthroats. Among the most notorious and dangerous of the lot were Bill Doolin and his gang of desperados. Wanted dead or alive, Doolin seemingly could not be taken.

Law enforcement, such as it was in the nations, ran out of Judge Isaac Parker's court in Fort Smith, Arkansas. Judge Parker's marshals actively pursued outlaw elements in the nations, rounded them up, and hauled them before the hanging judge for justice. Not Doolin. He slipped every encounter and, in several cases, left an intrepid officer of the court dead. Then Bill Tilghman cut his trail.

Tilghman picked up Doolin's trail and followed him to Eureka Springs, Arkansas, where he found him in a bathhouse. Bill caught the unsuspecting outlaw with his pants down, so to speak. Despite his embarrassed condition and the fact Tilghman had the drop on him, Doolin made a play for his shoulder rig lying on a bathhouse bench. Tilghman succeeded in buffaloing the man and subduing him without firing a shot — no small accomplishment where so many others had forfeited their lives for the same attempt.

With Doolin safely secured in Judge Parker's lockup, Bill returned to the nations, where the rest of the gang remained at large. By dogged determination, keen tracking, and guile, Bill conducted his pursuit of the Doolin gang members. He successively caught up with Bill Raidler and Tom Calhoun. Each resisted. Their outlawry ended in Tilghman's deadly gunplay.

"Little Dick" West became the last of the lot. Second only to Doolin in notorious reputation, he, too, had left a trail of dead lawmen who'd attempted to take him in. By the time Tilghman got through with the boss and the rest of the gang, "Little Dick" must have known what he was up against. He also knew he faced certain hemp justice if he were apprehended. He knew Tilghman was coming; it was only a matter of time. He determined to take his chances. He did. And he died.

John Henry (Doc) Holliday

As you know, I never cared much for Doc. There were good reasons. He had a certain Southern charm when the spirit moved him to display it, which wasn't often. I suspect the spirit frowned on strong drink, which

287

left little room for Doc's "charm." To me, his Southern gentleman came off as arrogant. About as sartorial as a fart. To his credit, he was an intensely loyal friend to Wyatt. You had to admire the way he stood by Wyatt and his brothers to even the odds at the O.K. Corral fight. Doc had no dog in that fight, other than friendship. He acquitted himself courageously. I could admire that. Faced his own death from consumption without fear. Of course, he may have had fear; he just hid from it in a whiskey bottle. He was drunk most of the time and mean tempered when he was. He gambled and whored, both pursuits that might earn a man enmity. Doc had a hair trigger that made him a killer. He packed a pair of nickel-plated, double-action Colts, a .41 Thunderer and a .38 Lightning. He was deadly accurate with either. Kate Elder loved him. God knows why; I suppose somebody had to. Wyatt called him friend, and, as I've said, that was enough for me.

Luke Short

I smiled in reflection. We've told most of Luke's story, though there are a couple things we could mention. Luke Short lived up to his name — five foot six and a hundred forty pounds. You wouldn't think a man that size would have survived very long in the life he led, but he did. He was split-second quick with a gun and fearless.

After our buffalo hunting days, Luke and a partner established a trading ranch up in Dakota Territory, just across the border from an Indian reservation in Nebraska. They had a nice business, trading ninety-cent bottles of whiskey to the Indians in return for ten-dollar buffalo hides. The Indian agent didn't approve. He called out the army to put a stop to it. They arrested Luke while his partner was away on a buying trip. They hauled him into Sydney, Nebraska, from where he would be sent to Omaha for trial. The whole town of Sydney turned out to see what sort of desperado required a whole troop of cavalry to corral. Luke's partner was there in the crowd. Luke's army escort and the crowd thought Luke might be daft when he started rambling on in Sioux. His partner understood.

The train for Omaha pulled out on time that afternoon. Luke was back in Sydney by nightfall, having jumped the train. He was fearless, which makes the last part of his story interesting. After gun scrapes in Arizona, Colorado, the Dodge City War, and another shoot down in Texas, Luke Short died in bed. Pretty remarkable accomplishment for a man like us; not many did. With a little luck, Wyatt and I may make it yet.

Ben Thompson

We've had our reminiscences of Ben right along. I am amused by an encounter he had in Abilene back in '71. I wasn't there. Ben told me the story. It makes me smile still. Abilene was the first railhead cow town. It sprang up far enough west to keep Texas Longhorns from infecting domestic livestock with tick fever. Ben and his partner, Phil Coe, opened a saloon they called the Bull's Head to accommodate the Texas trail hands. The Bull's Head and the rest of the so-called "Devils Addition" were wide open. Ben's gun hand kept a lid on his place. Coe, too, was competent with a firearm. The security detail completed when John Wesley Hardin took a shine to the place. Ben fed him drinks to keep Hardin coming around.

The Bull's Head didn't need extra security, but that couldn't be said for the rest of the town. The city fathers hired James Butler Hickok to pack a star and see to local law and order. Hickok had a good start on his "Wild Bill" reputation by the time he hit town. Ben and Hardin mostly had a live and let live respect for Hickok. Wild Bill and Coe had a rough spot over a woman, but things mostly stayed civil, with Ben and John Wesley backing Coe.

Ben's trouble with Wild Bill came up over a sign Ben had made to attract customers to the Bull's Head. The sign featured a big bull, standing on its hind legs, sporting a lascivious grin and a ready-for-anything monument to cupidity to go with it. The traveling Texans thought the sign humorous and flocked to the Bull's Head. The city fathers weren't amused by the sign. Indecent, they charged, as the reform minded are wont to do. If the city fathers weren't happy, then neither was Wild Bill.

Hickok called Ben out and told him the sign had to go. Folks all over town speculated almost from the moment Hickok arrived who might survive if it came to gunplay between Hickok and either Ben or Hardin. No one knew among that trio who might prove best. I suspect none of the three had an interest in finding out.

Ben thought over Hickok's ultimatum and decided to comply, sort of. He had the sign's offensive members carefully whitewashed in such a way they might be gone, but not forgotten. Hickok must have thought it over, too. The sign stayed, and no more was said about it.

Hickok and Ben never threw down on each other. Ben was out of town on business when the bad blood between Hickok and Coe boiled over. Coe got drunk one night and started shooting up the town. When Hickok attempted to disarm him, Coe made a play. He was dead before he hit the ground. In the commotion that followed, Hickok mistakenly killed his deputy and friend, Mike Williams. He cashiered his star over that and ended his career as a lawman.

Hickok was gone by the time Ben returned to Abilene. He never pursued Hickok over the incident. He figured Coe was a big boy and should have known better. Ben learned later Hickok was diagnosed with glaucoma. Some say Hickock's blindness was brought on by venereal disease. Either way his failing eyesight may well have contributed to his error in killing his deputy. A lot of people know the story of Hickock's death and the dead man's hand. Not many know his eyesight may have set all that in motion.

Metropole Hotel
Forty-Second and Broadway
Runyon shook his head. "You couldn't make this stuff up."

"You could, but no one would believe you."

"It's amazing as many as three of you lived to die of natural causes."

"Only one of us has made it so far."

"Yeah, yeah . . . I haven't seen you take down too many gun fights on Broadway recently."

"Wyatt's given up that sort of thing, too, according to all reports. I suppose that tilts the odds in favor of your point."

CHAPTER THIRTY-TWO

Shanley's Grill
Forty-Third and Broadway

We agreed to meet for dinner before heading over to the Garden to cover another card of aspiring contenders trying to catch enough lightning in a bottle to justify a title shot in the heavy- or middle-weight divisions. You had to cover those fights to keep your finger on the pulse of the game. They seldom offered serious surprise, but you could never tell when some new talent might emerge. As usual, I preceded Runyon to the appointed meeting, secured a quiet booth, and ordered my Manhattan before Runyon presented himself out of breath.

"Sorry I'm late. Usual excuses."

"Excuses accepted, as usual. Don't tell me; let me guess: the get-away car got away."

"Never go near the things. I have my reputation to consider."

"Reputation? I should think you'd first

reconsider your public associations, present company excepted, of course."

"Of course. You get your story material your way, and I'll get mine my way."

"At least my methods aren't likely to lead me behind bars."

"Mine haven't yet. For the record, I seem to recall you've seen the inside of a jail cell a time or two."

"Purely circumstantial."

"I'll claim the same. Remember, I never go near the get-away cars."

The waiter came to take our steak orders.

"Tell me something," Runyon said. "Did you never think of returning to the West?"

"To live? No. I've grown quite fond of civil society here in the East."

"Surely the West has grown civil by now."

"It has, though lacking in certain amenities."

"How do you know?"

"Alfred Lewis and I covered a heavyweight title fight between Jack Johnson and former champ Jim Jefferies in Reno back in 1910."

"Ah, Jefferies — the 'Great White Hope.' "

"Tex Rickard promoted the fight. Our train stopped in Dodge on the return trip."

"Got a fresh look at a settled old haunt, did you?"

I did.

I remember observing vistas of prairie and plains as the train rolled across Kansas. The territory of my youth, once wild and rugged, now domesticated to all manner of agriculture and peaceful pursuits. Fields and flocks, farms and livestock laid out in orderly, pastoral tranquility where once the buffalo and red man roamed free.

We'd started it all, of course, my pals and me. Dixon, Tilghman, Wyatt and his brothers. Not the agricultural enterprise. Tilghman did a little ranching, but none of the rest of us got anywhere near that calloused-hand, strained-back kind of work. We brought law and order to places where those who did agricultural, mercantile, and industrial things might prosper. We played our parts and passed on or moved on to be replaced by those better suited to building the things scrolling by the coach window.

The train stopped for a bite of breakfast at the Harvey House in Dodge. Thirty minutes of nostalgia. I bolted my bacon and eggs to make time for a walk. The old town had mellowed from those turbulent times. It now stood vested in civility as befit progress. There might be a tug at memory left for an old-timer like me, but progress waits for no man. Air that once stank of a mountain of buffalo hides or choked on a perpetual dust storm hovering over the cattle pens now breathed clean. At least it was still hot. I recall ducking instinctively at a loud report that accompanied a gunshot back in my time. This time it signaled a tin-lizzie backfire.

The storefront that once housed Chalk Beeson's Long Branch Saloon still stood, along with the old jail across the tracks where I last left it, the jail likely not doing so brisk a business as it did in those early days. They'd patched and painted over all the bullet holes we'd thrown at Peacock and Updegraff. I smiled at the idea of shooting up the town one last time. I suspected fines would have gone up some from the eight bucks it cost me the last time. I was pretty sure I couldn't find a city official with a familiar face to fix my disorderly-conduct charges. They were all gone now. Come to think of it, so was any semblance of disorderly in my conduct. I'd become the most orderly a man might imagine. Boring. Just old.

I thought of those who tramped these dusty streets in warm recollection. Short, Tilghman, Thompson, even Holliday and that scallywag Nick Klaine, who'd thrown in with A. B. Webster and the reform crowd. We'd made some history. Now Wyatt and I were the only ones left. In time, I doubted anyone would remember. Probably why I bothered to tell this story. Somebody should remember, before I get so old I forget myself.

The whistle blew "all aboard." I glanced around one more time to the realization it was one last time. I toed the dust with my shoe for good luck and boarded the train back to the present.

Morning Telegraph

The Telegraph did not confine itself to news and sports. Our sophisticated readership required more. Our society page covered the upper crust of the social scene with the occasional hint of delicious scandal always appreciated. We also covered the theater. These latter diversions were written by my colleague Louella Parsons.

Louella was young and pretty, fresh off her first journalistic endeavor with a midwest daily. She was fascinated by the theater. Like Runyon, she had aspirations to become a playwright, which she would eventually transfer to the moving-picture screen. I believe she did eventually sell a script, but her future and fortune remained in journalism, though firmly imbedded in her fascination for film. At *The Telegraph,* all of that lay in her future. She had the Broadway beat.

She insisted I see a Broadway production portraying the West called *The Barrier.* I had a hard time imagining a Broadway play set in the West, competing with the wild-West shows of the day. My friend Buffalo Bill Cody set the standard there, with panoramic outdoor settings done on horseback to reenact everything from Custer's demise to the Oklahoma land rush. The Western story, it struck me, was too big to confine to a stage.

After a week's worth of her nattering, I resigned my reservations. I took Emma, who enjoyed the stage, reminiscent of her own days treading the boards. I must confess, I went to the theater with low expectations, fully prepared to hate it. I didn't. The play starred William S. Hart. Hart made a believable Westerner. It may be that some of his doings reminded me of some of my own or those of my friends. We'd lived the frontier; it was daily life. I knew folks glamorized it and found fascination in what for us was simple survival. Dime novelists and writers like Alfred Lewis glorified the West in print for as long as the West existed in time or memory. Bill Cody discovered you could make a good living from people's willingness to pay for a taste of it. Here it was, then, on the Broadway stage.

Before long, Hart would put the West in moving-picture shows. It would become a marriage made in heaven. Hart knew the West; you could tell. He knew how to portray it believably even to one who'd had a part in it. The West lived on in pictures; a part of me lived with it. I didn't expect to appreciate it that much, but I did. We did that, didn't we? My pals and me, we did that. We'd all fade away. Memories would fade, too. Hart's pictures, like a Remington bronze or a Russell canvas, would not. Some of what we did and who we were would live on. I confess I liked that notion.

CHAPTER THIRTY-THREE

Madison Square Garden

We took a coffee break in the bowels of the Garden after the undercard. Runyon had a smoke with his coffee. How the man subsisted on a diet of coffee, cigarettes, and delicatessen fare I took for some marvel violation of nature or science. The main event for the evening had attracted a good deal of interest in a match between two promising contenders.

"I couldn't help but think we might see him here tonight," Runyon said.

"Funny, I had the same thought earlier this evening. I even forgot myself for a moment and peeked at the presidential box. It's the sort of match T.R. would have wanted to see."

"Hard to believe he's gone."

"It is." We fell silent while Runyon favored his cigarette and flicked at the ash.

"You were among those who urged President Roosevelt to seek a third term, were you not?"

"I was. He should have, too." I couldn't deny a bit of regret at that. What might have been? "I think T.R. came to see it that way, too, when Taft turned out to be a bloated empty suit."

"Is that how the Bull Moose Party came about?"

"That was some of it. The country was fractured; the political parties reflected that. Taft ran the gentrified, blue-blood, elite, Republican money crowd, but you still had reform minded progressive Republicans like me who backed T.R.'s brand of honest government. The Democrats weren't in much better shape. They had their own populist faction who didn't have much use for the milquetoast college professor Wilson. The whole thing was ripe for a barroom brawl. That's about what happened."

"You mean the three-way race."

"Yeah."

Runyon studied the rafters. "That seldom works out well."

"Oh, I don't know. We did all right by Lincoln winning a four way in '60. This one might have turned out O.K., too, if it hadn't been for that sniveling anarchist in Milwaukee."

"The assassination attempt."

"Not many men take one in the chest, get up, and deliver a stem-winder speech of over an hour."

"The president was fortunate for the length of his speech. As I read it, the written text folded in his breast pocket saved his life."

"Helps to be long-winded sometimes. That and a case for his glasses saved him. Too bad they couldn't save the election. Put him down for a couple of weeks in the teeth of the campaign. He still knocked the air out of that gasbag Taft."

"Gave the election to Wilson." Runyon crushed out his cigarette under a polished shoe.

"There is that. Couldn't be helped under the circumstances."

"Closed out the career of a great man."

"Sorry to say. He did that hunt down the Amazon and came home so sick and dissipated by tropical disease, he wasn't fit to take a command in the Great War a few years later. I can tell you this: things would have gone differently early in the war if T.R. had been in the White House. That pacifist pinhead Wilson had no spine. Couldn't bring himself to go to the aid of our allies until his ego needed a seat at the peace table to redraw the map of Europe. That appealed to his book smarts. He had no real stomach for the dirty work done by men of character in times of war. Thank God Pershing did."

I kind of lost interest in politics after Wilson won election. The voting public was so full of dopes, I doubted the country could survive much longer. Between the social reformers, anarchists, and dewy-eyed idealists with cotton for brains, you couldn't make sense of any of it any longer. At my age, it didn't seem to matter much anymore.

We drained our coffees to the clang of the bell in the ring. We tossed the paper cups in a trash can we passed as we returned to our seats in the press box.

CHAPTER THIRTY-FOUR

Toledo, Ohio
July 1919

Runyon and I were close friends. Some wondered why. He covered sports for Hearst. Baseball mostly. Some boxing. He had a special talent for fiction. Got a lot of his material from hanging out with the wise guys who ran New York's underworld. Somehow, he managed to walk the fine line between friendship and the right side of the law, at least most of the time. He got real close to the line with me over the Dempsey-Willard heavyweight championship fight.

We both lost money on that one. Damon on his "Manassa Mauler" and me on the "Champ," Jess Willard. I didn't think much of Dempsey; I thought him overrated. He was prominent among the yellow-bellied dodgers in the fight game who avoided military service during the Great War. I could not abide the unpatriotic display of cowardice by those who disported them-selves in the ring. I made no secret of my disdain to my readers. It heavily influenced my estimation of Dempsey, that and the questionable nature of the record he amassed on which he laid claim to being a heavyweight contender. If all that wasn't bad enough, Dempsey got himself tangled up with Jack Kearns for a manager. Kearns had all the charm of a rattle-tail reptile with a reputation you couldn't trust as far as the tip of his rattling tail. Boxing had enough ethical challenges without the likes of him.

It was common practice in those days for writers to take a spiff under the table from a manager or promoter to flog a fight or a fighter in their columns. I never did. Held a low opinion of anyone who did. I don't know that Runyon ever engaged in the practice. If he did, it never struck me so from reading his stuff. He made some bets, though. Well, we all did. The bet he made on the Willard-Dempsey fight took on something of an aroma in the aftermath of the fight.

Deserved or no, Tex Rickard signed Wil-lard to a title bout with Dempsey. The fight was scheduled for July 4th in Toledo, Ohio. Why Toledo? A sane person might ask. Because that's where the fight could be held without legal or political interference. That and the fact Ohio made a day's train ride from New York, less from Chicago. All of which fed Rickard's hope for a big gate. He needed it to cover the guarantees he had to put up to get Willard. Dempsey was hungry. Kearns smelled a big payday. By the time he got done with Tex, Rickard needed a big gate. The challenger's guarantee would have made a fine purse for an ordinary championship fight. Runyon and I were both there to cover for our respective columns. We ran into each other a couple days before the fight at the Willard camp. We'd come to watch the Champ work out.

"And how is the world's foremost authority on pugilism this evening?" he said.

I may have lowered a brow at the sarcasm. "Expert as ever."

"As I examine your record of predictions and wagers I wonder how you managed to achieve such notoriety. You seem to have missed all the big ones, most notably Dempsey."

"Missed him? What's to recommend him? He came on the scene having stolen the name of a prominent middleweight champion. He's managed by a charlatan who put him up to a procession of faux pugilists he knocked down like nine-pins. And this is the legend you anointed Manassa Mauler? Mauler indeed."

"Backward looking, all of it. I expect he'll do more than quite well against the title-holder you're backing."

"We shall see."

"Have you backed your conviction with a wager?"

"Five hundred to win, even. Have you?"

"Today. Dempsey in a first round K.O. at ten to one."

"First round K.O.? Even at ten to one, it's a sucker bet. Look at Willard: he's got height, reach, and near sixty pounds on your man. More than that, the Champ has never been down."

"Dempsey hits like a sixteen-pound sledge."

I didn't know it at the time, but there may have been more truth than hyperbole in Runyon's brash prediction.

July 4, 1919
Fight day dawned hotter than a firecracker on the Fourth of July. Oh, wait — it was the Fourth of July. Plenty hot, too. I pieced the puzzle of these events together after the fact, though I'll tell the tale as I believe it happened.

The fight drew more than the usual interest in a championship bout, including some on the shadier side of Runyon's acquaintance. Alfonse Capone came in from Chicago with his usual entourage of muscle. As events unfolded, someone among them, or maybe even Kearns himself, may have been the source of Runyon's ten-to-one tip.

Rickard had previously announced that the fighters' hands would be taped and gloves donned in the ring in plain sight of all. For reasons I never figured out, a Marine drill team performed between the undercard and the main event. They tore up the canvas such that it had to be replaced before the fight. That pushed the taping to the fighters' respective dressing rooms. Kearns showed up at Willard's dressing room to observe his taping. He returned to Dempsey's room to personally see to his fighter's taping. He was accompanied by Willard's corner man, who would observe for the Champ. Dempsey's room was crowded; Willard's man didn't have much of a view. His protests were stifled by the rough demeanor of some in the crowd. I made them Capone men by deduction, but nobody ever made that accusation, let alone prove anything of the sort.

The opening bell was still reverberating when Dempsey cut loose a left-right combination that felled Willard like a tree. Broke his jaw and knocked out a couple of teeth. Willard was tough. He beat the count, though he may have been out on his feet. Dempsey put him down six more times in the first in the most amazing display of punching power I've ever seen.

The last time he went down, the place went nuts. Kearns jumped into the ring somewhere around the seven or eight count when Willard showed no sign of getting up. He raised his arms in the air, dancing with delight. Runyon threw his straw boater in the air. Big Al lit up a fresh cigar, and all the ten-to-one, first-round K.O.'s counted their killings. The celebration went on until the referee finally got control of the situation to announce the bell had rung on the nine count, and the fight would continue. The joint broke out in another round of howls, this time in protest. No one had heard the bell for all the commotion. It didn't matter to anyone, other than to those holding the ten-to-one bets.

Willard was game. Battered as he was, he lasted four more before his corner called the slaughter off. A new champ was crowned. The boxing world was abuzz with Dempsey's punching power. No one had ever hit Willard like that before. It didn't smell right from the beginning. A first round K.O.? Who in their right mind would have predicted that? No one. Who would take that bet? No one. That's how you get ten-to-one odds. When I started hearing whispers about the taping, I became convinced Dempsey entered the ring that day with loaded gloves. The damage done Willard was murderous. Most of it on his right side, courtesy of Dempsey's left. I never called it out in my column. Everyone knew I'd backed the Champ and lost money. With no proof, it would only just sound sour grapes. The only consolation I had was the ten-to-ones lost a bundle, too.

I have to say that, along with my losses, I was disappointed in Runyon. He had a piece of the action in what smelled like a fix. We talked about it the next time we broke bread.

Shanley's
Forty-Third and Broadway
"Why?" I said.

"Why what?"

"Why'd you take ten to one on a first round K.O.?"

"Ten to one. Wouldn't you?"

"The other side. It was a sucker bet . . . unless."

311

"Unless what?"

"Unless the fix was in."

"What are you saying?"

"I'm saying Dempsey's mitts were loaded. At least the left one."

"I don't know anything about that. It's pure speculation anyway. If you thought that, why didn't you up the jig then and there?"

"I didn't find out about the taping irregularities until later."

"What irregularities?"

"Willard's corner never got a good look at what went into Dempsey's gloves."

"His hands went in. They came out, too."

"The only ones who knew what went into those gloves were Dempsey, Kearns, and some wise guys who had a piece of that ten-to-one action."

"I don't know that. What makes you think so?"

"I heard."

" 'You heard.' That prove anything? If it did, you could have scooped your suspicions in your column."

"Everyone knows I had money on Willard. I'd a' been blown off for a sore loser, and, as you say, there's no proof. Still, I wonder."

"Wonder what?"

"Did the smart money tip you off on the bet?"

"What smart money?"

"The money smart enough to know it wasn't a sucker bet. Who told you?"

"I don't remember."

"Smart."

"Smart as not printing an accusation you can't back up."

"That angle never crossed my mind. I know those boys make great fodder for your stories, but I'd be careful if I were you, Damon. This time all it cost is some money."

"And would have given me that ten-to-one, first-round K.O. if the bell no one heard hadn't saved your about-to-be-dethroned champ."

"Was it worth an outcome that should have been no less tainted than the one that ensued?"

"Speculation. Nothing more."

"A dark stain on a game sometimes prone to such stains. A swindler wears the crown, and his partner in crime counted the winnings."

"Forgiveness and forgetfulness — two of the qualities I admire in you most, Bat."

"Can't say I've ever been accused of either before."

CHAPTER THIRTY-FIVE

Metropole Hotel
Forty-Second and Broadway

We got over the Willard-Dempsey fight. I made my point. I doubted I could break Runyon of his hoodlum habit as it related to the legitimate purposes of his writing. I satisfied myself he'd think twice before exposing himself to another fix-tainted fight. We all make mistakes when we're young; heaven knows I surely did. Listening to myself sounds like wisdom; I must be getting old.

A couple weeks later Runyon showed up at the Metropole Hotel after work, looking to make amends. I ordered a Manhattan. Runyon, his coffee and a cigarette.

"Remington, Russell, and Hart. Bronze, canvas, and film. Your West. Do the arts record it justly?"

I had to think. Runyon had a way of picking at my sentiments. I never had many you could get at so easily before we started reliving my journey. Must be my age again.

"That's a deep question."

"We try."

"The artists you mention do. Each in his own way."

"How do you mean?"

"Remington captures the physical power and emotion it took to tame some small part of the West: a bronc, a steer, a raucous band of cowboys, even a prideful red man. Russell captures the big picture: the color, the grandeur, the vistas."

"And Hart?"

"Hart takes up where Buffalo Bill left off. Bill Cody's wild-West shows gave people a taste of the West, a taste Eastern folks hungered for. The shows were spectacles. Near as big as life itself. Expensive, too. Too expensive to survive, as it turned out."

It struck me then the passing of Bill Cody's wild-West shows marked yet another legend passing.

"When it comes to legends, they don't get much bigger than Bill Cody. I met him back in the day. Knew him well enough he helped me get Billy Thompson out of his Ogallala scrape. Cody made his legend killing buffalo. When the buffalo were gone, he turned his notoriety into a wild-West show. He made a new legend out of the old ones. I don't know how he did it. I mean I know how he did it; it's putting up with the how of it I could never figure out. Neither could Hickok or Sitting Bull for very long. Both appeared in Cody's shows. Sitting Bull lasted longer than Hickok. I suspect Wild Bill's time may have had something to do with his eyes. Sitting Bull was comfortable being part of the spectacle. Had a soft spot for Annie Oakley. Called her 'Little Sure-shot.'

"Buffalo Bill did it up grand. Saw him in New York not long before he passed. He was an old man then, but he still had that showman's fire in his belly. Talked about taking over a failing show and putting it back on the road. I remember thinking, moving-picture shows had put his extravaganzas out of business; he just didn't know it yet. Probably best he never found out."

"So, you say Hart's films pick up where Buffalo Bill left off. When did you meet him?"

"Couple of years ago. He dropped in at *The Telegraph.* He was in New York promoting a new film. He'd heard I was in New York and wanted to meet me. I suspect Louella was behind it. By then she'd taken herself off to California to cover the movies for Hearst. Hart proved to be a delightful man with the soul of a Westerner, no matter he hadn't actually settled the West.

"We had a nice visit. He befriended Wyatt in California; we had that in common. He explained how he'd tried to convince Wyatt to appear in one of his pictures. Wyatt refused. He could be curmudgeonly that way at times."

"Wyatt could be curmudgeonly." Runyon laughed.

"What's funny?"

"That accusation coming from you."

I suppose he had a point. "Takes one to know one. Now, where was I?"

"Hart tried to convince him to appear in a picture."

"Oh, yeah. Wyatt did agree to consult on a few of his productions. Hart asked if I might consider appearing in one of his films. If I did, it might get Wyatt off the dime. I couldn't picture a Western film being enhanced by the portrayal of a comfortably plump old gunslinger and said as much. He laughed. Told me we'd both underestimated people's appetite for our notoriety. Maybe so. Then again, has been, has been. I saw no need to resurrect that past. We posed for a picture or two, had a little lunch, and said our good-byes. Nice fellow. I wish him luck."

"I hear stories about you and Hart. I can't figure out which one of you was the bigger fan."

"A little bit of both I'd say. I admired his work from the first time I saw him on Broadway. He could play the part of a Westerner square. He has enough of the right stuff in him to make it believable. You could drop him in Dodge with some of my old pals, and I expect he'd have fit right in."

"I read that piece he wrote about you for *The Morning Telegraph* back in '18. It sounded like he was the fan. Thought the world of you and Wyatt Earp plain enough."

"He did. Bill liked having Wyatt around. I think knowing us some helped him with his parts. He portrayed characters that did things like some of those we got up to."

"Seems like there was more to it than that."

"Well, maybe. For his parts, Bill felt a powerful connection to the history of the West. He said Wyatt and I had a hand in making that history."

"He had the right of that."

"I admired what he was doing, too. He was laying down on film a record that would survive long after all of us were gone. He was like the film version of Russell and Remington. Those boys had their art; he

318

had his."

"He kind of dismissed that in his article. Called himself an imitator of the real men of the West like you and Wyatt."

"Imitator? Maybe, but you had to be believable to pull it off. Bill Cody's shows were imitations, too. They were good because he lived it. Took in folks like Hickock and Sitting Bull when he could to add to the authenticity. Cody's shows didn't last. They were over when the tents folded up for the last time. Bill Hart's films will live on, longer than any of us."

I ordered another Manhattan near out of sentiment. Time for a perfecto.

CHAPTER THIRTY-SIX

Lundy's Delicatessen
Broadway, New York

Every now and then he'd talk me into his deli. I'd no more than get my butt warm on a bench with a soggy sandwich, and I'd start kicking myself for letting him do it again. Resigned, I waited. As is his habit, Runyon hurries in from Broadway, passes an apologetic nod in greeting, and bellies up to the counter to place his order. He plunks his purchases down on the table in a ruffle of wrappings, paper napkins, and coffee steam.

"If you are going to keep me waiting, might we at least do it in a civil dining establishment?"

"What's uncivil? This from a man who once ate his meals prepared over a fire made from dried buffalo dung."

" 'Once' was a long time ago."

"And Lundy's is a long way from dried dung."

"Depends on who you ask."

"You are becoming an impossible curmudgeon, Bat."

"I prefer to think of it as experienced."

"There's no accounting for taste," he said around a bite of his tuna salad on rye.

"Taste from a man with a mouthful of sandwich relished in coleslaw."

He dabbed at his lips with a napkin. "It's really quite good. You should try it."

"I'd rather prefer to change the subject."

"Of course. All right. After listening to all of these stories, it strikes me that between you and your friends, you are the history of the West. Did that ever cross your mind?"

"Not in so many words. We did witness a lot of history, though."

"More than witness; you made it."

"Some of us did."

That began to settle in with a letter I received from Bill Tilghman back in 1911, as I recall. Quanah Parker had died. Bill visited with him shortly before he passed to the land of his grandmothers. Parker told Bill the story of Adobe Walls from his side. I didn't grieve for the man. He was Comanche after all. Back in the day he'd have eaten my heart, given the chance. I take that prospect personally. I thought better of bringing the subject up over lunch. I couldn't risk Runyon putting coleslaw on it. Still, it was a passing of the old days. I took a little nostalgia from the story as he told it to Bill.

"Bill Tilghman once got the Indian side of Adobe Walls from Quanah Parker shortly before he died."

"Really. Tell me about it."

"We cut ol' Quanah and his war party up pretty good with our big fifties. They took heavy losses from those long guns and some boys who knew how to use them. We held 'em at a range from which they couldn't reach us. Somebody even put a heavy through him. Nearly sent him to his ancestors then and there we did. Nearly."

I played over Tilghman's letter in my mind. One thing led to another.

"Billy Dixon left us next. He made an end of the Adobe Walls fandango with the longest shot I've ever seen. Even Billy allowed as how there was some luck to it, but you don't draw that kind of luck without a passel of skill to back up the invitation. Parker and his bunch tucked their ponies' tails between their checks and lit out after that one. Billy Dixon was one savvy man. I do believe that bunch of buffalo hunters put more hurt on the Comanche in three days than the army reprisal did in the eighteen months that followed. I expect Billy'd be right proud of that wherever his camp is pitched now."

"What happened to Parker after the war?"

"Quanah Parker moved his band to the nations in Oklahoma. They were dirt poor like most reservation Indians. Parker was smart, though, I'll give him that. The Comanche had one thing that might be made to profit them."

"What was that?"

"Land. Parker figured out he could lease grazing rights to the big Texas ranchers. He persuaded the tribal elders to go along. The tribe prospered, and Parker became personally wealthy. After the war he earned himself notoriety and respect."

"How so?"

"Like I said, he was smart. Had a head for white ways, courtesy of his white blood. He learned to read and write after the war. They used their grazing money to build schools and educate children in the ways of the white road.

"Parker helped launch tribal businesses in ranching and farming. He invested in railroad building and became a savvy politician, known to Washington leaders including President Roosevelt. Through all of it he managed to preserve many of the old ways and customs. He was instrumental in establishing a Native American church. He used the church along with reservation sovereignty to preserve customs like polygamy and the ritual use of peyote. He had his seven wives and twenty-four children. They lived in a twenty-four-room mansion known as the Comanche Whitehouse."

"Rather an amazing fellow."

"He was."

"Seven wives? It's illegal."

"I told you Parker was smart. The reservation was sovereign territory. Tribal elders made their laws. They practiced the old ways for religion where it suited their purposes and used the white man's laws to their benefit when and where they saw fit."

"I'm surprised you ever defeated them."

"I'm not sure we did."

CHAPTER THIRTY-SEVEN

Shanley's Grill
Forty-Third and Broadway

We ordered our usual steaks accompanied by coffee. I flavored mine with a surreptitious splash of Old Crow from a flask I'd taken to carrying in my inside coat pocket. I rolled my eyes at the indignity. Who would have imagined a civil society come to this. Runyon lifted a brow, amused. I read his expression; I'd put him in mind of something.

"Over the years your writing seldom wavered far from sport, boxing in particular. Now and then you indulged in moments of remembrance with your pals in the West, but there is one other topic in which you vigorously wet your pen."

I had a feeling I knew where this was headed. "You mean politics?"

"Politics certainly entered into it. I'm talking about your enthusiasm for reformers."

"Enthusiasm. Is that what you call it? You mean those loathsome hypocrites who prey on our lives and liberties out of the misbegotten notion they have some higher moral standing from which to do so? I have no tolerance for reform foolery, if that's what you mean."

"That seems a rather broad condemnation. Your friend T.R. was reform minded."

"That's different. T.R.'s reforms were aimed at government intrusions on the lives and liberties of the governed. He fought abuses of the sort purveyed by Tammany Hall, not the self-righteous, moralistic bilge spewed by our self-appointed betters. Just which steaming platter of bovine pie brought this to your attention?"

He chuckled and shook his head as though my response were wholly predictable. I sensed he'd goad me further. It annoyed me to admit I'd not disappoint.

"Let's see."

He thought.

"Yes, some of your more defensible and understandable tirades were waged against boxing reform."

"What's to defend? The pugilistic arts are manly sport. Period. Man has engaged in physical contest since we dropped down from the trees or crawled out of the slime, whichever theory of origination suits you. A little sweat, a little blood contested to the finish between two able combatants; where, pray tell, is the harm in that? The sport is conducted under civilized rules. No one dies in the main. And, if some should choose to wager on the outcome, how does that cause injury to any holier-than-thou moralist who is under no obligation to so much as observe such a contest? In fact, we should all be far better off left to the pursuit of our own enjoyments. But no. The reformer cannot abide the notion of another man taking pleasure in a pursuit the reformer finds offensive to some genteel sensibility known only to him, or worse, her. For that, I should be denied the liberty of my pursuit? Rubbish!"

"And so you have said, steadfastly and repeatedly. But, don't you admit, the bare-knuckle London prize ring game was . . . verged on the barbaric."

"Barbaric to you, perhaps. Tough and manly to those who engaged in it and those who saw sport in it. What made the reformer right and the sporting man wrong?"

"The Queensbury Rules were adopted for a reason."

"And, did that quiet the howling ninnies? No; nothing ever does. The nanny ninnies never have enough."

"The suffragettes came next."

"Oh, that."

"You can't possibly argue against a woman's right to equal protection with men under the law."

"Why not? Women prospered famously for centuries without it."

"Some would question your claim of prosperity. Enlightened times called reform forward."

"Enlightened. Weak minded men badgered by their womenfolk, you mean."

"Too bad Emma isn't here to hear you opine."

"That genie is out of the bottle. There is no point to further discussion."

"Of course not."

He smiled as though he had me stymied on the point. I suppose he did when he inserted Emma into the conversation. Matters political are seldom tidy. I simply couldn't let him have the last of it, though.

"And what did we gain from advancing the franchise to the gentle sex? Votes to heighten demand for further reformation upon individual rights and liberty cast in the guise of temperance. Not merely temperance, mind you. We contort the constitution to prohibit man the comfort of spirit.

What founding father would have ever condoned such nonsense?"

"None of course. Do you suppose there is a whisper-in-a-sawmill's chance free men would deny themselves the comfort of strong spirit? I grant you, allowing the fair sex the vote surely contributed to Prohibition's passage. I'll not debate the right of the franchise, but you've only to pat your pocket to remind yourself your right is not wholly abridged."

"Fine for you to say, my coffee-drinking companion. You're not the least bit inconvenienced by the fact the personal liberty now concealed in my pocket might serve to put me in jail if observed. What if the next reform were to ban your use of tobacco?"

"Come now, be serious."

"I am."

"There were plenty of men who advocated for the Eighteenth Amendment and the Volstead Act."

"Men? Gasbag politicians fearful of their wives and the clerical hypocrites who exploit their purses on Sunday mornings. You call those men? Nary a one would have survived so much as a week in the West."

"Oh, come now, Bat. Western men were well represented in the Prohibition movement."

"Men who grew up with gaslights under hard won law and order. It's all a load of hokum. You think Prohibition works? Let's finish our meal and walk around the corner to the speak-easy, shall we? There we can have civilized drink of poor quality at exorbitant prices, secure in the knowledge we are contributing to the ill-gotten gains of the criminal element who prey on society. The only amusing aspect to all this balderdash is that the criminal element in politics willingly surrendered their ill-gotten sin taxes to the even more ill-gotten gains of the underworld." I had him there, indicted by his own associations. "So then, I ask, what has all this high-minded reform gotten us?"

"Sorry I asked."

CHAPTER THIRTY-EIGHT

Broadway and Sixty-Sixth
Thursday, October 26, 1921

I hurried through the early evening gloom. The streets were thronged as offices and shops disgorged their staffs at the end of the day. They scurried off to homes and families, gatherings with friends, and social engagements. Automobile engines, exhaust fumes, and horns mingled with the clop and clatter of horse-drawn coaches and wagons. A brisk autumn wind snaked along the cobbles, propelling a flotsam of leaves, paper scrap, and snippets of debris. Mellow gaslight faded into the shadows, beaten back by the advances of brilliant electric light. I paid no mind to any of it in my haste.

I bounded up the red carpeted steps to the front entrance and shrugged out of my coat. I tossed it at the check-desk attendant, pocketed the token, and made my way inside. The crowd had already begun to thin as I crossed the large room framed in dark wood, exchanging nods and glances with mutual acquaintances and friends. The air was warm after the evening chill, vaguely scented of furniture polish, candle wax, and a hint of some indistinct floral sweetness. I found a seat at the far end of the room.

He waited patiently. I was late, of course, and braced for some glib barb, poking at my lack of punctuality or disorderly life-style. None came forth. I nodded in greeting, wondering what turn his story might take tonight. His mood seemed sanguine; I took comfort in that. Wherever his thoughts, he seemed in no hurry to continue his narrative.

We sat in silence for some time, savoring somewhat more companionship. I spoke of my latest short story, one I thought showed promise. He listened thoughtfully. He could always be counted on to encourage pursuits he judged beneficial to me, reserving his occasional disapproval for those sources I sometimes turned to for material. I had in him a character. A character of whom he would undoubtedly disapprove, but a character that suited him nonetheless. I smiled at the prospect of what he might say, should he come to the realization he and Nathan Detroit had something in common.

We fell silent, along with the room. After a time, the lights dimmed until only the candles stood vigil. My eyelids grew heavy, restful in warm comfort. My chin nodded. I must have dozed off. I sensed it first. Something tugged me alert. Shadows processing out of the darkness. Could it be?

The first apparition stood beside him, head bowed, slouch hat in hand, shoulder-length black curls curtaining his eyes. The Sharps big fifty cradled in the crook of his arm seemed out of place here in the city, though not unexpected. He raised his gaze to the horizon. Something there caught his eye. Oddly, I recognized a stranger I'd never seen before. Billy Dixon met my eyes, nodded unspoken recognition, and passed on.

A second figure stepped forward with a nod to me and took his place beside him. He carried the Sharps of another buffalo hunter. A star on his vest caught candle light. A Colt slung on his hip. Bill Tilghman paid his respects in confidential whispers. I'd have given anything to hear what they said. A man of few words, the conversation was brief. He, too, went his way.

Charlie Bassett came next. I recognized him from the tintype. Round featured, a little on the portly side, lips moving silently over some likely memory of Dodge. A crystal tear trickled from his eye. An old man's sentiment. His eyes met mine, affection there, and he, too, was gone.

A dapper dandy next doffed his derby hat, coat brushed back behind double-rigged Colts. He leaned close for some silent exchange beneath a neatly trimmed moustache. He chuckled at some shared humor. Ben Thompson looked to the darkened ceiling, shook his head, and bid his friend *Good show.*

Broad-brimmed hat swept low in a bow. The buckskinned showman in knee-high boots, white haired and mustached, cut a figure larger than life. Larger than life? Indeed. All of it real, and none of it life. He stood head bowed, hat in hand, to honor a man he called friend.

The shrunken cadaver who next approached coughed into a handkerchief. Pearl-gripped, double-action Colts shoulder rigged cross draw announced their presence behind a dark coat. Doc Holliday shuffled a deck of cards in one hand, cut the ace of spades, and showed him. He dabbed at one eye and stepped by.

The next little fellow from the tintype needed no introduction. He laid one hand on the burnished wood beside him, shook his head, whispered of some shared remembrance. Who could say what? They'd done a lot, the two of them. Made a peace commission statement over the Dodge City War. Had each other's back more than a time or two. Then, Luke Short, too, took his leave.

The gumshoe William Pinkerton next approached in dark suit, starched collar, and tie. He paused only briefly before, glancing around the room, pocket watch in hand, he hurried off on some urgent errand.

The Lewis brothers arrived together. William and Alfred. Publisher and author. Employer and friend. He owed them both much. A byline and the reputation he valued so. I believe he thanked them again. They for their part nodded him welcome, enriched for having known his friendship.

Candle light reflected wire-rimmed spectacles. Could it be? The bully, toothy grin of a Rough Rider in morning coat. He stood, hands clasped behind his back, head bowed. What passed between them, I cannot say. Perhaps they spoke of some appointment suited to a new day. He patted his hand in farewell, hunched his shoulders resolute and strode away.

Hart. I'd heard he might come. So serious his expression, sorrow never far to go. He came with his friend, to call on a friendship shared. He paused but briefly out of respect for the moment that would follow his.

Wyatt stood tall and lean, ramrod straight in spite of his age, troubled by something in his eye. He stayed with him for some time. I watched his lips move. I strained to hear what they said; I could not. I suppose that proper. It would have been unseemly to eavesdrop on murmurings between old friends, sharing such a time. Stay with him, friend. It pleases him you are here.

I sat in awe of all I had seen. History played out before me, a voyeur privileged to peer into the past through the eyes of those who were there. I must have dozed off again while Wyatt was with him. When I awoke, he was gone. The candles guttered, feeble light going out. My eyes fluttered. Gray light filtered the silence. I rose from my hard-backed chair and joined the end of what had been so distinguished a procession.

I stood there with my friend for a time. Quite a story. You saved the best for last, old friend. All of them here to pay their respects. I can scarcely imagine how proud you must be. You said once something to the effect, as a gambler, you expect to break even. Well, for one last time, Bat Masterson beat the odds. You go out a winner. I let my tears fall. They were all I had left.

Morning came to collect me. October

twenty-seventh. Two days since he finished his last column at his *Morning Telegraph* desk. His last words to a colleague that morning, "I'm all right."

"All right" indeed. That day we laid him to rest in Woodlawn Cemetery. William Barclay Masterson was sixty-seven years old, one month shy of his sixty-eighth birthday.

IN HIS OWN WORDS

Bat Masterson died at his desk October 25, 1921. The following was found in his typewriter.

"There are those who argue that everything breaks even in this old dump of a world of ours. I suppose these ginks who argue that way hold that, because the rich man gets ice in the summer and the poor man gets it in the winter, things are breaking even for both. Maybe so, but I'll swear I can't see it that way."

— *W. B. Masterson*

Courtesy of Wm. B. Masterson, a.k.a. Jerry

AUTHOR'S NOTE

The events of Bat Masterson's life and those of his friends as recorded here are historically accurate as best we could establish the record. Historical records being what they are, there may be fine points to dispute, but, at least where Bat himself is concerned, we counted on two impeccable sources, biographer Robert K. De Arment and Bat Masterson impersonator Jerry W. Eastman. When I set out to write this book, I imagined Bat telling his story to a star-struck cub reporter. It was only after I began researching the book that I discovered his relationship with Damon Runyon. Runyon was no cub reporter, but he and Bat were indeed close friends. They say the character Nathan Detroit in Runyon's classic Broadway hit, *Guys and Dolls,* is based on Bat Masterson. In fact, Runyon did spend the night before Bat's burial in the funeral parlor with his remains. Years later he reported an experience that night, something akin to the one we imagined here.

— Paul Colt

ABOUT THE AUTHOR

Paul Colt's critically acclaimed historical fiction crackles with authenticity. His analytical insight, investigative research, and genuine horse sense bring history to life. His characters walk off the pages of history in a style that blends Jeff Shaara's historical dramatizations with Robert B. Parker's gritty dialogue. Paul's first book, *Grasshoppers in Summer,* received finalist recognition in the Western Writers of America 2009 Spur Awards. *Boots and Saddles: A Call to Glory* received the Marilyn Brown Novel Award, presented by Utah Valley University. To learn more visit Facebook @paulcolt author.

The employees of Thorndike Press hope you have enjoyed this Large Print book. All our Thorndike, Wheeler, and Kennebec Large Print titles are designed for easy reading, and all our books are made to last. Other Thorndike Press Large Print books are available at your library, through selected bookstores, or directly from us.

For information about titles, please call:
(800) 223-1244

or visit our Web site at:
http://gale.com/thorndike

To share your comments, please write:
Publisher
Thorndike Press
10 Water St., Suite 310
Waterville, ME 04901

CPSIA information can be obtained
at www.ICGtesting.com
Printed in the USA
BVHW032329200220
572958BV00001B/18